Charm Offensive

William Thacker

Legend Press Ltd, The Old Fire Station,
140 Tabernacle Street, London, EC2A 4SD
info@legend-paperbooks.co.uk
www.legendpress.co.uk

The right of the above author to be identified as the author of this work has
been asserted in accordance with the Copyright, Designs and Patent Act
1988. British Library Cataloguing in Publication Data available.

ISBN 978-1-9098785-3-2

Set in Times
Printed in the United Kingdom by TJ International
Cover design by Gudrun Jobst www.yotedesign.com

Legend ▌Press

Independent Book Publisher

Author and Scriptwriter **William Thacker** was born in London in 1986. He is a graduate of Lancaster University (English Literature with Creative Writing BA) and the University of Manchester (Creative Writing MA).

Since 2009, William has written scripts in partnership with Manchester-based Honlodge Productions whilst working as a professional copywriter. In 2013 he co-wrote his first short film, Full Time, which has been screened at film festivals in the UK and internationally.

William is currently working on his second novel and is developing a feature film script. He lives in London.

One

You can say what you like about him, but you'd probably do the same. In his defence, he has never tried to be a saint. He is aware, painfully so, that he has no explanation.

Around town, his name has become a byword for how to kill a career. Don't do a Joe. It's why he lives in a smaller house now, with white-painted roughcast walls and a mattress on the lawn.

At the door, Muriel slides the chain free.

He has hung about her, successfully, for longer than predicted. He has remained an occupant of the house, still married, despite everything.

He allows his voice to be heard.

'They're satisfied.'

'Okay.'

'You do believe me, don't you?'

Just by stepping into the house, you can tell that something has been lost. It feels like the morning after a burglary, like someone has come inside and wrecked everything.

He will clean the mess he is responsible for. He should reposition the cushions. But when it comes to the broken glass - that's Muriel. The dent on the door is Muriel. The mattress on the lawn is Muriel.

She is keeping her distance, in her white nylon dressing gown and white slippers. On most days, a black camera is wrung around her neck. Today there is nothing.

She is resting her elbows on the kitchen counter, staring

from the window. Her collarbone is pronounced. It's a bony smile across her chest.

'I haven't done any work,' she says.

'I was going to ask.'

'No you weren't.'

Then she motions for him to turn around. She says that his shirt is inside out.

There is a question that he can't put into words. He could try.

'What do you want to do?'

She turns from the window and says, 'Why don't you have a bath?'

If it wasn't for him, she might not sigh so often. She might still look young. Her hair might be long and dark, not short and grey. She might be more prolific in her work, more confident, more sociable. He has made her old.

*

Muriel is sitting in bed with the duvet pulled around her shoulders. She must have spent most of the day like this. It's hard to imagine that she's done anything else.

The curtains are closed.

She has avoided the en-suite bathroom, where the hanging wire, chemicals, photographs and light sensitive materials are kept.

'I should probably go.'

'Alright.'

In his imagination, it was going to be a front door goodbye. It was going to conjure some emotion. It's not happening like he thought it would.

'I'm going away for a bit.'

'Am I supposed to say something?'

'No.'

She won't follow him. For now at least, she won't be moving.

It's true that some of her anger is justified. After all, what started all this trouble? It was the finer things, the finer women. But on this occasion, she's wrong to assume the worst.

'You don't have to say anything.'

'Alright.'

'I know it's hard to believe me. I haven't always been… faithful.'

'True.'

'But this is different.'

In the absence of something more to say, there is silence. It's impossible to live in a silent house. Instinct says it must be a bad idea.

*

In their neighbourhood there is little of interest. It takes five minutes on foot before you reach the roundabout and its patch of grass. Best of all is the iron bridge, which no-one likes to walk across. You have to tread carefully to avoid the broken glass. And the dog shit.

The pub has broken windows.

What can you say about the beach? Unlike most beaches, no-one is having a good time. The most you can say is that the view is something to admire. No-one can take away the hills in the distance.

It's possible to make out Barry, leaning on the sea wall. The car will be parked in front of the souvenir shops. Barry is pointing at his wrist, doing his best to hurry the whole thing along. Just relax, Barry.

There is an old pier, which is beginning to look fragile. There are tables at the pavilion, some seagulls, and a mean-looking flag hanging from a kiosk. On the deck is a black chalkboard, and the words are beginning to fade.

Tonight: a conversation with Joe Street,
former Member of Parliament.

You would think someone might have erased it. It would be easy to change the sign, but no-one will make the effort.

From the pier, you can hear the tide wash over the stones of the shore.

There is a parade of candyfloss traders.

A dodgems circuit.

Crazy golf.

On the concrete walkway is a shed where the pedalos are kept. Further along is the lifeboat museum.

There are cranes from where the shipyards used to be.

You can just make out a tanker in the distance.

There are seagulls overhead, circling the sky, crowing for someone to throw something. Don't they know that no-one cares?

He stares out to sea. If he were a seagull he would shit on the town.

Two

By the end of the week, everything will be fine. All he needs to do is sort out the trouble. Sort out the lie. That way he can make a plan for freedom.

No matter where you look – be it the petrol station to the left, or the business park to the right – there is nothing you would call beautiful. If you hadn't visited for years, you could be misled into thinking everything is better now. A social revolution in the form of plastic apartments.

'I'm excited,' Barry says with his hands on the wheel. 'For the first time in ages people are talking about Joe Street.'

'For appalling reasons.'

'Do you even know the girl?'

'No.'

The best thing is to clench the seat belt cord.

On the dashboard is a tabloid rag, which Barry must have bought, as if to demonstrate his idiocy.

'Bastard thing,' Barry says, shifting into fifth gear.

The car is an enemy. The car is something to resent, and pity. The car is an idiot.

When you look at Barry, there's a temptation to pull his cheek, just to check it's not a rubber mask. Aside from their heads, which are balding, they have nothing in common.

'I think it has become professionally advantageous to acknowledge the girl.'

'For something I haven't done?'

'The public likes honesty. That's as much as anybody can

be these days. Honest and kind.'

'But I am being honest.'

'Not in their eyes. They like a man who's keen to build bridges.'

'I haven't broken any bridges.'

'You're paddling.'

*

This is a crisis and he knows it too well. You don't book a hotel room above the Hanger Lane gyratory system without there being a crisis.

Hanger Lane, in outer west London, is the sort of place you'd visit if you don't like London very much. There is a tube station if you need it, and a motorway, which allows a quick exit.

The sound of passing cars can be heard through the pane. What is there to see? Eight lanes of traffic and a tube station. Somewhere in space, alien creatures will be looking down and laughing at Hanger Lane. Of course, when you look out of the window it's hard not to have one of those moments where you think, what am I doing here? The reality is too much to think about. And for a man of his age – fifty-nine – there's only so much time in which you can keep fucking around.

On the floor is a cardboard bucket filled with grey chicken bones.

A piece of the remote control is missing, which requires him to hold in the batteries whilst changing the channel.

On the television is the rolling news. Watch it for long enough and you'll lose your mind. It's the highlights from a debate in parliament. The volume is too low to hear anything. They will probably be talking about the war, and the reasons for sending combat troops. Even without the sound, you can see the cabinet members frowning. Some of the opposition are waving sheets of paper. The speaker of the house bangs the gavel.

'Order, order,' the speaker will be saying.

If he were there, on the backbenches, he would be shaking his head. By the time he had left Westminster – or rather, been told to resign – he was an irrelevance. That was four years ago. It was a conventional sort of disgrace. And of course, it was a legitimate scandal, unlike the one that has since befallen him.

'Would you send troops?' Barry says.

'No.'

'It's a shame you can't vote.'

On the next channel is a game show in which the contestants make fools of themselves.

Barry opens his laptop on the desk. 'We need to stick something on your blog.'

'I don't want a blog.'

'Yes you do.' Barry fixes something on top of the monitor. 'Just speak into the lens like it's a real person.'

'What do I have to say?'

'Talk about how the internet is transforming the way young people engage with politics.'

'That doesn't sound like me.'

'I know. Here, look at the screen. Do you see your face?'

'Is it on?'

'Yes, go ahead.'

It's difficult to know where to begin.

'Hello. I'm Joe Street.'

His voice seems weaker than he expected.

'I don't want to sit here and tell you what to think. It's important for people to decide for themselves what they believe. I just hope everyone can be the person they want to be. Just… be good. Don't kill anyone.'

'That was weird.'

'I don't have anything else to say.'

'Don't kill anyone? Let's do another take.'

'No.'

'We're recording.'

'Turn it off.'

'Good afternoon, Joe. What did you think of the Prime Minister's speech today?'

'I think he's a cunt. Turn it off or I'll smash that thing on the floor.'

'Calm down.'

'Turn it off, then.'

It was all supposed to be simple. If it wasn't for the lie, he could do what he wanted.

There is a stapled document on the bed.

'What's this?'

'It's got everything I need to know. Your successes, your failures. I need to update the section on failures.'

'You'll need a lot of paper.'

Joe Street, former education secretary. The fallen minister. The lost politician.

Barry walks to the window with his hands on his hips.

'The kid runs a soup kitchen. He's a do-gooder type. You must know the sort.'

'I am the sort.'

'George, he's called. A do-gooder.'

'You said.'

'Born with a silver spoon in his mouth. His parents gave him some money to set up a homeless charity.'

'That's nice.'

'A guilt complex, I'd call it.'

If he looks at the floor, he won't have to debate anything. With any luck, Barry will see something funny on the television.

'I've thought about what you should say,' Barry says. 'You should be cagey.'

'Cagey?'

'You should leave open the possibility that it might be true.'

'I'm not doing that.'

'Only a glimmer. You don't have to hold your hands up.

We just want to keep the cycle going.'

'Why?'

'It's a strategy. You can't go from pariah to prince in the blink of an eye.'

'I don't want to be either.'

Barry is frowning, as if there is nothing to be done about Joe Street. A lost cause or something.

'I've seen it all, mate. The amount of Joe Streets I've called and they've said, 'Barry, get me out of the papers.' You're in good company.'

It's true that Barry has built a career in damage limitation. He's cheap, as well.

Barry straightens the duvet cover. 'Remember, this is a charm offensive. A branding exercise.'

'What should I say?'

'Don't speak about anything negative. It's a happy occasion.'

'Will I meet the homeless people?'

'You should position yourself as close to them as possible.'

'So I just hang around and hope there's a camera?'

'Got it.'

There is nowhere to go. In front of him is the window, the motorway and the miles of traffic. There is no escaping any of it. You can't exactly jump out of the window and ride on the back of traffic.

'Did you remember to moisturise your face?' Barry says.

'No.'

'Just remember next time.'

*

Cutting Corners, which calls itself a hair and beauty salon, is positioned between a bookmakers and a shop that sells ink cartridges. You could set up a good business in Hanger Lane, simply for the fact that so many people pass through it. Cars are allowed to dominate.

If you ask Barry, a haircut is not just a haircut. It's of the utmost importance. It's the next piece in the jigsaw, and no doubt the following piece will be just as important. What will it be? A manicure, or something.

'Have you decided what you want?' Barry says.

'Do I have a choice?'

'You want to look like a pro. Do you know what I mean?'

'No.'

The hairdresser brings a cup of tea, which she places agonisingly out of reach on the near shelf.

'What can I do for you?' she says.

'I think,' Barry says, pausing to examine the hair, 'it should be short. Maybe an inch or two.'

'I could take the weight out of it.'

'Yes, but keep something on top. Don't make the bald spot too obvious.'

'Is that okay with you?' she says.

It's funny to see Barry interrupt himself, as if to acknowledge his own guilt.

'Yes, of course. What do you want, Joe?'

'Short is fine.'

'I think it would look nice short.' The hairdresser pulls the length at the back.

'Short and professional,' Barry says.

She points towards the washbasin.

It's no surprise to see Barry follow, but a disappointment all the same.

'Lean back,' she says.

In theory, it should be simple to lean back in the chair and rest your head in a washbasin. What makes it complicated is his inability to position his head in the right position.

'A bit lower,' she says.

The best thing is to close his eyes.

Barry must be standing somewhere.

It's nice, all of a sudden, to feel the hairdresser work her fingers into his scalp. It makes him forget about everything.

'You recognise him, don't you?' Barry says.

'Please, Barry.'

'He's a politician.'

'I'm not a politician. I used to be.'

'He was one of the good guys. Do you remember the campaign to save shipbuilding in Hartlepool?'

'No.'

'That was Joe.'

She is doing things, all the while. She is adjusting the temperature. She is listening.

'How do you know each other?' she says.

'I got a call from Barry. There was something written about me.'

'Was it bad?'

'Yes.'

She twists the tap screw. The water doesn't flow anymore.

She holds the white towel on each of his temples.

'Stand up.'

The embarrassing part is the walk from the washbasin. He probably looks like a dog coming in from the rain.

The hairdresser lifts his arms into a black robe, fastening the strap across his neck. On the counter is the cup of tea, although he isn't sure what to do with it. One hand is free, the other is under the robe.

With mirrors on all sides, it's easy to see the back of his head. His hair is thinning, and almost grey. He has been complacent about his face. It's not that he's ugly; in fact, if you leave aside his age, his impression to the world is of a handsome man who just doesn't care. It's more the fact that he can no longer conceal his sadness. At least he's got something to work with - a firm jaw without a double chin, and enough life in his eyes so as to give the impression of kindness. Of course, he doesn't bother to work with it. To hell with it, right? It doesn't matter what you look like. Yes, he has become complacent.

*

When they get to Hammersmith, everyone seems delighted about the sunshine. It's a national event - sun at last.

The shelter is based within a Georgian townhouse. It's a listed building, and you wonder what its original purpose was. The plaster is crumbling. There are iron bars covering the basement window. You get the feeling it will be worth a lot in ten years, when the gentrification is complete.

In the main hall is a crowd of people. Some of them are journalists. The key is to avoid them like you would a crab. If you keep your distance, the crabs will leave you alone.

You can't tell who the homeless people are. Barry is looking for them simply by scanning his eyes over the room.

'I'll tell George we're here,' Barry says, as if the big boys are in town.

'I didn't expect there to be this many people.'

'I find it exciting, don't you?'

'No.'

Everyone is working on something. A couple of teenage boys are carrying chairs. Even the journalists are pulling out the table.

Someone rises.

'Take a seat,' George says. 'Thanks for coming down.'

It's hard to square the George in front of him with the George that Barry had described. There is nothing to hate. George is young, perhaps too young to be running such a thing. Something in the region of twenty-five, twenty-six. What are the clues? The mop of auburn hair; the pimples around the mouth; the straight back, yet to be crippled by sitting in front of a computer for eight hours a day. If anything, you almost worry for George. There is plenty of time for George to lose all hope. It will come.

'Welcome everyone,' says George, who is wearing a buttoned-up shirt with a neat collar.

There is enough space at the table. It's long and white,

similar to what you would find in a school canteen.

A photographer picks up what looks like a golf bag.

The journalists follow.

'Eden House serves fifteen to twenty-five people a night, most of whom are homeless, or struggling with their finances. Most of our food is donated by local businesses.'

One or two of the reporters are jotting notes.

'We offer counselling and medical information,' George says. 'We rely on volunteers and patrons. And of course, any publicity you guys can create is a real bonus. It would be wonderful to have the support of people like Joe.'

'And Joe is delighted to be here,' Barry says.

'Indeed.'

The reporters crowd closer together. Each of them has a name tag pinned to their chest. There are tape recorders and notepads.

'You've had a tough week,' the *Ealing Gazette* says. 'Tell us what it's been like.'

'Tough.'

'Why have you come to a homeless shelter?'

'I thought if I could speak on a platform, and tell the truth, it would undo some of the damage.'

'Is it just a cynical attempt to paint yourself in a better light?' says another reporter.

'I don't know what it is.'

'Have you spoken to Margaret Eccles?'

'Yes.'

'What does she think?'

'She's satisfied. It's a non-story.'

Barry has been waiting for his moment. At the first opportunity, Barry will intercept the silence.

'Joe's a fighter,' Barry says. 'Whenever he gets knocked down he's always back on his feet. I'm sure Joe won't mind me saying he's learnt a lot these past four years. He's had the time to build up a thirst for social justice once more.'

'Will he be back?'

'Oh, certainly. It's only a matter of time. He was telling me just the other day how liberating it is to spend time with ordinary people.'

'What do you think Joe?'

'About what?'

'Barry said you have a burning desire to get back into parliament.'

'That's not a description I recognise.'

'Tell us about your ambitions. What keeps you going?'

'I want to help people.'

'How?'

'I'm figuring it out. Right now, my ambition is to clear my name. Then I can live out my life.'

'And that's it?'

'That's it.'

The Harrow Observer tears off a clean page.

'Let's take you back to the events of last week. How did you feel when the Helen story came out?'

'I was… '

'Aghast,' Barry says. 'Put aghast.'

'Joe?'

'I'm happy with aghast.'

The Willesden Herald opens a file and pulls something out. It's a newspaper cutting.

'Do you regret anything?'

'What would I have to regret?'

The silence is filled with the pouring of water.

'It's a pretty serious accusation.'

'Yes.'

'And if proven, it would demean everything you've ever stood for.'

The newspaper cutting is there, dangling in front of him.

'You built a reputation on helping the less fortunate. How does it make you feel when people say, 'great, he's nice to strangers but he won't look after his own disabled daughter.''

'I've got one daughter. She's twenty-nine. And nondisabled.'

'Where were you when Helen was born?'

'I don't know.'

He could tell them a lot about Helen, without having met the girl. He could even describe the nature of her disability in better detail than the journalists could. If you're meant to have done something wrong, you might as well research what it is.

The Hounslow Chronicle says, 'Are you going to sue?'

'I don't know. Someone has just put two and two together and come up with a fucking nightmare.'

It's only at this point that he's satisfied enough to fold his arms and lean back in his chair, although he can't be sure that it won't fall.

'Has your reputation made things worse?'

'Can we talk about something else? Everything you've heard is wrong. The rest is history.'

'But can people believe you?'

'Yes.'

'Does your family believe you?'

'That's enough.'

A camera flashes.

Then he puts his hand on the table where the journalists are sitting. All of them are looking up at him. Some of them look worried that he might be offended; some of them look satisfied.

The Kilburn Times says, 'I understand you've launched a stunning attack on the Prime Minister, Joe. What's your reaction?'

'Excuse me?'

'Let's take a time-out, shall we?' Barry says.

'I'm going.'

The next challenge is to negotiate a way free. There's not much space between the tables. There are lots of obstacles to overcome.

The only person to get up from his seat is George. 'Cheers, Joe.'

'Sorry about this.'

'Thanks for coming.'

There are too many things to think about.

It's important to think about the distance between the table and the exit. It's only a few steps.

If he hurries, Barry might lose the scent. Barry might disappear.

*

'It went well, I thought,' Barry says on the way back to the hotel. 'What did you think?'

'I hated it. I found every minute of it utterly degrading.'

'Seven out of ten, maybe.'

*

In all the rush, it's hard to remember how they got back. The shelter... the taxi... the shouting in the foyer. It's hard to remember how they entered the hotel. It was an automatic reflex, as if their legs were moving like pistons, independent of the mind. Somehow they had pressed the button in the lift, and arrived at the bedroom.

'We should have gone back,' Barry says.

'You're an idiot.'

'I didn't mean to upload it.'

'Why did you say those things you know are untrue?'

'I'm trying to save your career. Is this your way of saying thank you?'

'You're in this for yourself.'

'Why did you sit there and say nothing?'

'I've got nothing to say.'

'You made me look like a fool.'

'You did that on your own.'

Barry raises a finger, the kind that says you need to be careful. 'If you're happy to live like some washed-up has-been, fine. You should be a lot less cocky considering everything that's happened.'

'Why's that?' he says and pushes Barry on the shoulder.

'Because you're the one with the case to answer,' Barry barges him back.

'Do you want to say that again?'

Their arms are locked together in a kind of rugby scrum. Their feet are treading on the magazines.

'I'm warning you,' Barry says.

Barry was supposed to be cuddlier than this.

In the grapple, it's hard to know what to do. It's like wrestling a bear.

Then it comes.

It's harder than he expected. It happens so fast that he's unable to think.

With his right hand, he feels the bridge of his nose. There is something to worry about. It's only now that he's conscious of the blood.

More than anything, he would like to close his eyes. He would like to sleep. The important thing is to avoid a kick to the head. You wonder how far it will go.

By the time he has roused himself, and found the courage to look between his fingers, Barry is standing in front of him. Barry says nothing and his face is impossible to interpret.

Barry reaches across the desk, retrieving a tissue from a box. 'I told you,' he says.

He is conscious that Barry is passing a tissue. You have to respect Barry for checking he's still alive. Should he say thank you? It would be strange to thank someone for punching you on the nose. He must thank him another time.

*

The dot of blood on the pillow is what makes him go to the bathroom. The nose, much as he expected, is beginning to soften. It's nothing to be proud about. It's certainly not a battle wound. It's punishment for being an idiot. It means that every time he looks in the mirror, he'll remember what a fool he is.

On the mattress is the document. The first page is what Barry has called an executive summary. It reads like something from the internet. You only have to read the first sentence to understand what the struggle is all about.

Joe Street (born in Goole, 1944) is a controversial former Labour Party politician who was a Member of Parliament between 1979 and 1999.

On the next page is a picture of him. The hair is thicker and darker than now. It has a diagram, labelled with words like 'idealistic.'

It mentions his core beliefs, some of which no longer apply. It has an entire section devoted to unilateral nuclear disarmament.

On the next page it says:

Margaret Eccles (born in Eastbourne, 1955) is a British Conservative Party politician. She is currently the Shadow Secretary of State for Defence.

It mentions the affair, and the events leading up to his resignation. Depending on your viewpoint, there is something shameful, or satisfying, about sleeping with the enemy. It's true that he had the affair, and that Margaret, Shadow Home Secretary at the time, was a disturbing kind of conquest - a Conservative with a fetish for sombreros. It's unfair though, that his name has been smeared in this latest piece. It was always going to happen. Someone was probably making notes. The story was already being written.

There is a section named *Helen Eccles*. It doesn't have an image, but there's enough information. From his own research, he knows it's not as simple as giving her a label. Not everyone belongs to a category.

He doesn't want to read anymore. It will only make him sad.

Three

It was a toss of a coin, in effect, about whether to visit the hospital, or whether to ride the tube. In the end, he reasoned that he might very well collapse on the tube, in which case someone will carry him to the hospital. You can kill two birds with one stone.

There is something exciting about getting on the tube without knowing your destination.

He is one of a small number of passengers to board at Hanger Lane. A couple of them are guests from the hotel.

Given that his nose is so bad, he doesn't want to make eye contact with anyone. Does anyone recognise him? Maybe one in twenty. Even if they did, they would be too polite, or scared, to ask anything.

Just opposite is a mother carrying a baby in her arms. Did the mother just look at him, or did he imagine it? If he thinks about it too much, it will disappoint him.

He closes his eyes and leans back, listening to the train moving. What's nice about the tube is that it rattles along, making it difficult to speak aloud and be heard. This is good, because it disguises the fact that no-one would speak anyway.

A part of him would like to stay on the tube until it reaches a terminus. By that time, he will have decided what to do with his evening. It doesn't seem likely that he could spend much longer alone.

It's a relief when the doors open and the passengers begin to exit. A new set of passengers will get on the train and stare.

Despite his nose, he's not the biggest story in the carriage. Sure, a couple of people are looking at it, but there is also a gentleman just opposite, who is frowning in his sleep and smells like beer.

It hadn't occurred to him that his nose would panic anyone until someone taps him on the shoulder.

'You alright, man?'

'Yes, thanks.'

'What happened?'

'Someone hit me.'

'Shit, man.'

'It's alright.'

Then he decides that he doesn't want to sit on the tube any longer. He gets up from his seat when the train pulls into Shepherd's Bush station.

*

The priority upon exiting the station was to find a Burger King. This was an immediate triumph.

He stares into the mirror. The empty burger tray is stuffed with bloodied tissues. He finds some blood under his fingernails. It will keep coming back to his attention, sometimes in the taste in his mouth, and sometimes on the specks on his collar. Some of the blood around the nostrils is beginning to harden. Someone should take a picture.

Joe Street, former education secretary. The fallen minister. The lost politician.

*

What does he do? He doesn't want to retrace his path from the station.

It begins to rain, which is quite unfortunate. Imagine his face. It will be covered in blood and rain.

He wonders for a moment what exactly he's doing in

Shepherd's Bush. It seemed like a good place to visit.

He walks inside the first pub and orders a beer. He doesn't bother to make small talk with the barman. If he sits on the barstool for long enough, someone will talk to him. Someone will speak. You would think.

In theory, he's doing a good impression of a sad, lonely man at the bar. It's not a good thing to be. It's not a good thing at all.

He orders another beer.

The drink will make him feel numb. He would like to feel numb.

The barman continues with his job, which is to retrieve beer, and exchange it for money.

He would like to say cheers, but it would sound like he's talking to himself.

After twenty minutes he orders another. The barman is almost reluctant to pull the pint.

'What happened to you then?'

'I got in a fight.'

'Did you win?'

'No.'

Would it be stupid to drink some more? Actually, he likes the idea. It will allow him to talk. He could introduce himself to a stranger. A stranger might laugh and buy him a drink.

Would it be weird to sit at a table in the hope that someone might talk to him? Maybe 'weird' is too strong, although it's probably not normal.

There is a stool at the back of the room where he can sit. A football match is being shown on the big screen, where most of the people are gathered. He is conscious that he's alone.

Then he is approached by a woman.

'Oh my god!' She points at him and says, 'I wrote an essay on this man.'

She introduces herself as Lauren and says she's studying Political Science.

The men watching the football begin to shout louder.

It's difficult to hear what she's saying, but he can make out some of the words. She says that she knows all about him, because she wrote her dissertation on peace movements. She says, too, that he shouldn't worry, because she doesn't care about his personal life.

'That's good to know.'

'Not at all.'

She had confronted him so quickly that he barely had time to register what she looks like. She is wearing a dark green cardigan and has big earrings somewhere beneath the mass of tousled hair. She's pretty, and it's strange that she's talking to him.

Her friends are standing by the quiz machine, talking among themselves. They don't seem interested in making an introduction. In fact, one of them is standing on tiptoes, trying to watch the football above everyone's heads.

Lauren is now completely apart from her friends, who are not even listening.

'You basically sold out, didn't you?'

'How do you mean?'

'You became like the rest of them. Before you resigned, before all that. You gave up on socialism.'

It's harder to hear what she's saying after this. The shouts from afar, and the groans of anguish, threaten to disrupt their rhythm. She is leaning over, half-holding her mouth as she talks. She says something about career politicians.

'You lost your way,' she says. 'I used to have so much respect for you, because you had principles. You were the last of the old guard. Then you sold out!'

'That may be the case.'

'You seemed so grumpy,' she says. 'You never seemed happy at the end.'

'To be fair, I didn't do myself any favours.'

'The Margaret Eccles thing. Yeah, she seemed like a bitch.'

'She was alright.'

'That's for another conversation,' she smiles, suggesting

the mood is still friendly, despite the anger and the punishing words.

Then she introduces him to her friends. One of them is putting money into the quiz machine. The other is sending a text on his phone. A couple of them mumble a hello.

'I quoted Joe in my dissertation,' she says. 'He was anti-nuclear weapons.'

'Oh, cool,' is the collective response.

And soon the conversation moves onto films, and most of it goes over his head.

The bell rings for last orders.

'Let's get something,' she says. 'Are you in, Joe?'

'Sure, go on then.'

As a group, they decide to order vodka shots and, on her suggestion, a bottle of white wine to share.

She leans on the counter and orders the drinks.

Then he wonders what to do. Should he speak to Lauren's friends? No, it's better that he waits with her at the bar.

'I suppose I'm glad you left politics,' she says in a confiding way. 'You can do more good doing... wait, what do you do now?'

'Nothing.'

'Oh,' she says, receiving her change. 'I'm sure you do it well.'

She pours some wine into his glass. It's like the good old days, talking about socialism and drinking white wine.

'Do you ever think you should be doing something worthwhile?' she says.

'Sometimes.'

She mentions how she volunteers at a school for children with learning disabilities.

'You see, this is what I mean,' she says. 'You're a textbook politician. You swear by the words of dead philosophers. You're not interested in people's lives. You've had decades to make a difference and what have you got to show for it?'

There is nothing to say.

'All that power and so much wasted time,' she says. 'And you're supposed to be the good guys!'

'It's not as easy as you think.'

'It makes me angry. Why don't you start afresh? Commit yourself to something.'

'Like what?'

'I dunno. Set up a charity. Volunteer. Protest. Do something!'

It feels like she wants to shake him by the collar until he pleads mercy.

'What happened to your ideals?' she says, talking louder than before. 'If you've given up, what hope is there for anything?'

'I'm not sure.'

'You could do so much more. Do something!'

She brings the shot glass to her lips. She leans back and lets the vodka sink down her throat.

It's difficult to know whether she's obnoxious or intelligent, or both. She is happy to speak her mind, which is important. She will continue shouting until the wine takes hold, and the words will no longer be so precise.

'So what are you going to do?' she says.

'I don't know. I don't have much energy.'

'You're not a marathon runner. You're not a nurse!'

'You're standing on my foot.'

What she wants is a passionate response. It's not something he can give. Perhaps twenty years ago he would give it a try. These days, he would rather be a punchbag. Whoever wants to step forward can gladly punch him.

'I don't understand people like you,' she says.

'Look, I've thought about it.'

'You've thought about what you're going to do?'

'Yes.'

'And what is it?'

'I haven't decided yet.'

She is looking around the room as she laughs, just in case someone heard it too. 'You haven't decided?'

'No. It'll be something worthwhile, though.'

'I look forward to hearing about it.'

When she speaks in this way, he leans more towards the opinion that she's obnoxious. She is at the summit of the moral high ground, waving from the top as he flounders at the foothills.

If he says nothing and continues to sip his wine for a moment, she might realise how obnoxious she is. If he tries to make an argument, she will attack his words.

A feeling of regret, for the years that now seem wasted, consumes his whole being. Just by listening, you get a sense of what he has become. Without knowing it, he has fashioned an image of himself as an old, tired goat. It's depressing to listen to this student of politics, whose words cause precise harm, and whose expression is of someone who's just trod on something.

'I'm sorry if I'm being over the top.'

'It's fine.'

'It's just tabloid junk, isn't it?' she says, referring to his name in the paper. 'They shouldn't be so hurtful.'

'I don't mind.'

'You're a good man, really.'

He allows himself to smile. 'Perhaps.'

*

They walk out into the street.

'Your nose,' she says under lamplight. 'I didn't realise it was so bad.'

'Yes, it's bad.'

He wants to lean on the bus shelter. This reveals to him, after a moment's thought, that he's drunk. He has been drinking too much.

'Are you alright?' she says.

'Yeah.'

She offers him a cigarette.

'No thanks.'

'Maybe you should see a doctor.'

'I might do. I haven't decided yet.'

She is pulling a face that shows she's listening and smoking at the same time.

The drinkers are outside with them. Among the drinkers, there is no-one that looks older than him. There is an unspoken age limit of about 40-years-old. He has smashed the limit.

The ritual, then, is to stand in the cold, and wait for something. You get the feeling they will be standing here until the landlord comes to shoo them away. What makes it even stranger is to see everyone smiling and laughing. What is there to smile about? People are hugging each other, as if to celebrate something. Then he wonders whether he should simply enjoy it. This is life, Joe. This is young life, smoking in the night, and never wanting to go home.

Lauren throws her cigarette on the pavement and treads on it. 'We're going to a club,' she says. She doesn't take the sentence any further. 'Are you going to be alright?' she says.

'I'll be fine.'

It's harder to focus on her words. He feels, even more now, that he would like to lean on the bus shelter.

In the corner of his eye, Lauren's friends are gesturing for her to come along. They have already begun to walk. If she doesn't hurry, she will lose them.

'Well, it was nice speaking to you,' she says. 'I'm going to look out for you.'

Then he mumbles something along the lines of yes, please do.

'Are you going on the march?' she says.

'I think so.'

'Great. I'll see you then!'

There is a moment when neither of them know what to say. She leans over and kisses him on the cheek.

'Goodnight.'

'Night.'

*

For some reason, he hadn't made a plan for tiredness. Where does he go now? Can he stay awake? It's getting late and his nose is beginning to hurt. His main feeling is tiredness, above all else.

He is walking, and it's better to keep staring ahead rather than look over his shoulder. It must have been twenty minutes. The thought of getting on the tube, when he feels so sick, and tired, and drunk, doesn't feel like something he can do. No, it would be better to keep walking in the rain. The good thing about the rain, of course, is that it washes off the blood.

It feels like he has been walking for a mile, perhaps longer. Admittedly his sense of distance is skewed, somewhat, by his drinking. It wouldn't be a surprise to learn that he has been walking for five minutes.

Then he wonders whether he should lean on a lamppost. Not to worry, Joe. Keep going! This is what happens in the night. This is what ambulances are for.

Wouldn't it be odd if he had nowhere to sleep? Wouldn't it be terrible if he slept in a park? That's where he's heading now, Ravenscourt Park, the Hammersmith end. Hammersmith! He knew he would remember it from somewhere. He remembers Hammersmith because this is the place where he met George and the homeless people and did the interview. Yes, that's the thing he remembers. Is it too late? He checks his watch and increases his speed along King Street. Yes, it's the building he remembers, Eden House, just before the Hammersmith flyover. George will let him stay.

It all begins to take shape in his mind, stepping through the door and into the hall. The canteen-style tables are at once familiar. Some young helpers are putting away the last table. Some other lads are sitting on the stage playing cards.

Where is George? George must be somewhere. It would be nice to see George, if only so they could have a cup of tea. Is he well enough to see George? It's important to be on good form. He will be speaking to George, no less.

There, coming out from the corridor, is George himself.

George, in his knitwear and chinos, is like a catalogue model for middle-class suburbanites.

'Joe?'

'I got lost.'

'Your nose... '

'Yeah.'

Then he remembers, once again, that he's drunk.

'You won't tell anyone, will you George?'

'No, I won't tell anyone.'

'I feel a bit sick.'

Then he tells George that yes, he has been drinking, and he wants to sleep.

'Come on,' George says, and puts his arms around him. 'Come with me.'

They begin to walk down the narrow hall, which has the feel of a school corridor. You half-expect to see macaroni pictures stuck on the wall. Lots of white paint has been applied over the bricks and pipes.

'Come on,' George says. 'Let's get you to bed.'

'I'm sorry. I'm an idiot.'

'No you're not.'

'I am.'

'I wouldn't help an idiot, would I?'

'You might.'

*

'You can sleep in here,' George says, opening the door to his office.

The office has a filing cabinet and a desk. On the far side is a sofa on which there are books and newspapers.

'Here you go,' George says, lifting some books from the sofa.

George apologises for the lack of a spare bed. There is no need to apologise.

George lifts a wastepaper bin, emptying the contents.

'Here,' he says.

It's tempting to stare into the bin.

Now that he's sitting down, it feels like everything is spinning out of control. He would like to sink his head into the bin. He doesn't want to look at anything.

George fills a glass at the washstand. 'How are we doing?'

A murmur will suffice.

'Have some water,' George says, bringing the glass closer. 'You'll feel better.'

'Okay.'

Then he can feel a damp cloth on his nose. George is holding the cloth.

'You should see a doctor in the morning,' George says. 'You don't want it to get infected.'

A part of him wants to explain how it all happened. How did it happen? The fight... the pub...

'I'll leave you to it,' George says, moving towards the door.

'Thanks.'

'Goodnight,' George pulls the light.

The door shuts.

There is a hole in the wall, which someone has stuffed with newspapers.

The sofa is small and has a loose spring digging into his back.

It was a smart idea, to think of George. It's important to have people like that. He must thank George, but it's late in the night and George will be going to bed. He must thank him another time.

Four

Hampstead was just a back-up option somewhere in his mind, something he would consider if hard luck or injury should befall him. He thought he should give it a try. As a rule, he wouldn't bother unless it was a crisis. This, his life at the moment, he considers a crisis.

He exits the tube station and takes a left at the high street.

It's true that he never fully understood Rosalind. He has a vague understanding of her personality; he knows she is artistic and opinionated. This is something to admire.

They might still be friends if only she wanted a father. It has been four years since they last saw each other, and he remembers the occasion well. She nearly lost her voice. It would be nice if this time was different. There's a lot to lose when you've only got one daughter.

Her home is halfway to Belsize Park, an area which blurs between tree-lined streets and a coffeehouse strip. An urban village, as the guidebooks might say.

It takes him longer to find his daughter's house than he'd expected.

The house is the same as he remembers, with a TV satellite on the roof, shutters to keep out the cold, cameras trained on the street, wrought-iron gates, reinforced windows, a conservatory round the back, and now, with the neighbour's home demolished, the space for a swimming pool.

He opens the front garden gate with his bag slung over his shoulder.

It's impossible to stay calm when he's under this pressure. It's the feeling you might get before a job interview. There is a big margin for bad things to happen.

Perhaps the sight of him will stir some sympathy.

It's better to treat it like a surprise. Sure, he could have called in advance. It's doubtful, though, whether Rosalind would have agreed to see him. If she opens the door, she will only have a moment to make the decision. She can't exactly turn him away. She will make him a cup of tea at the very least. Of course, the brightest idea is to expect nothing.

Is anybody home? There is music coming from the living room where Keith, Rosalind's husband, is sitting with a laptop on his knee. It's true that Rosalind could never afford to live here, were it not for Keith. An artist's salary isn't really a salary at all.

There is still time to run away, even as Rosalind's slight figure emerges from behind the front door glass. He could make an excuse. He could pretend he's sick.

He feels he should explain himself when Rosalind, who opens the door in a hurry, looks at him with no emotion. She doesn't even give a false flash of happiness.

He leans into her, receiving no hug, just the sensation of being pressed against crossed arms. He doesn't possess the skill of courtesy, and neither does his daughter.

'Oh,' she says aloud, with her hand on the door.

Then she calls into the house, 'It's alright, it's no-one.'

She doesn't call him Dad. She has no way of addressing him because she has no word for father.

There is nothing to say.

He feels the urge to raise his finger and say, I've done nothing wrong! But he doesn't say anything; in fact, he's silent and still.

When she looks at him, her expression changes in front of his eyes.

'What happened?' is the next thing she says.

'Someone hit me.'

She puts her hand on his shoulder. Then she pulls it away. 'Who was it?'

'My spin doctor.'

His eyes are looking for where her lips might curl.

She turns her back and says, 'Let me get you something.'

*

He had seen the house at the time of purchase, which was just over five years ago. Since then, the layout of the kitchen has changed to accommodate a retro fridge. Compared to when he last saw the house, it feels more complete. It has a long wooden dining table where someone has laid salad pots from Marks & Spencer. On the wall is a large clock without any numbers. Just opposite is a painting by Klee. They wanted a large home, which is what they got. It has enough space for a family, which is what they want.

Rosalind comes over with a hot damp cloth.

He can't help but notice how much Rosalind looks like Muriel. A slip of a thing, or however you would describe it. Her arms are on show, pale and thin, in a light spring dress. Her nose is small and straight. You can tell she has been painting, given the flecks of paint on her wrist.

'Stay still,' she says. 'Are you sure you shouldn't see a doctor?'

'It's just swollen. Ow.'

'See, it's split the skin.'

She seems to maintain a guarded caution. Why, if she's happy to dab his nose with a cloth, does she look so ashamed at doing so? It's her kindness that, despite everything, leads her to dab his nose.

'What have you been up to?' she says, just like a nurse might distract you with a question.

He mentions the story about Helen, in case she hadn't heard. It was important to kill the elephant in the room. It's the only way to move forward. No more elephants.

Rosalind is nodding in a way that suggests she knows all about it. She didn't want to mention it.

'Don't worry,' she says. 'I have very low expectations of you, so nothing you could do would surprise or disappoint me.'

'Nothing?'

She gives a quick glance. 'Nothing.'

It's true that he ought to explain a couple of things.

He says it was a lie, which is the truth. He says that Muriel might not believe him. Is he speaking too fast? Rosalind had asked him a simple question and he took it as a cue to ramble.

Rosalind is not going to say anything. She is silent, even in the pauses between his words.

Then he recalls the story of how he got here. Barry... the pub... the homeless shelter. It was a branding exercise Barry had arranged. But it didn't work. It didn't work because he's sitting here with a sore nose, and a daughter who looks more concerned than when he started talking.

'So why are you here?' she says.

There is no reason why he should be sitting here, which is why, slightly louder this time, she repeats, 'Why are you here?'

'I need a favour.'

'Really?'

'I just need somewhere to stay.'

Then he mentions the idea of meeting the journalist. It will put a full stop on everything. It will make a difference.

'And then what?'

'I'll go away.'

She applies the cloth against his nose as if she were putting the finishing touches on a painting.

'Look up,' she says.

Then he can feel the cloth against his nostrils.

'I spoke to Mum,' she says. 'She's going away for the weekend.'

'Where?'

'Weston-super-Mare.'

'Is she alright?'

'I think so.'

It sounds like he's making Muriel go mad. There is no pride in the fact. Muriel will be alone, in a small guesthouse, in Weston-super-Mare. You can feel the guilt coming.

'Did she mention me?'

'No.'

Keith, who is wearing a knitted beanie hat when he enters, says 'ah', as if to feign some pleasant surprise at seeing his father-in-law.

'How are you doing buddy?' Keith says, despite not being American.

'Good, thanks.'

'Cool, cool.'

Keith pulls out the chair at the table. Keith is about forty-years-old, which is eleven years older than Rosalind. Keith is a music producer. A pair of headphones are almost permanently wrung around his neck.

'Would you mind driving him to the doctors?' Rosalind says.

And Keith says, 'Sure, sure.'

*

'Cigarettes,' Keith says outside, feeling the pockets of his jeans. 'Okay, let's go.'

The car is exactly what you would expect of Keith. It's a convertible, with a light blue finish. It has parking sensors, and other things that make a small difference.

Keith doesn't mention the car, in the way that certain types of people won't draw attention to their wealth. You're supposed to think there's something natural about Keith driving a convertible. The car is incidental. It's simply a reflection of his brilliance.

It would be funny to be sick in the car. It would be worth it, just to see what Keith would say.

Keith starts the engine. 'You alright man?'

'Yeah.'

'What you up to these days?'

'Just living. Existing.'

'Cool, cool,' Keith says and turns on the radio. 'Do you like being in London?'

'It depends on my mood.'

'I love London,' Keith says, as if London were a homogeneous thing, like water or soil.

You can never imagine Keith complaining about anything. Everything is good. Nothing is bad.

'Yeah I'm still producing,' Keith says in his dry, smoker's voice.

Keith explains that he's working with a singer.

Then Keith mentions a couple of singers who are probably famous. You know they must be famous, because Keith's talking about them.

'I've been looking at writing a blog,' Keith says. 'Have you got one?'

'No.'

'Just stuff I like, that sort of thing.'

Keith, in his tailored vest, peers through the windscreen like he's suspicious of the road.

A teenage girl is walking across.

'Hurry up, fatty,' Keith says.

Keith has one hand on the wheel. The other hand is rubbing his stubble.

It's difficult to know what to say. The problem is that Keith is not someone who will tolerate silence. Your job is to say things aloud, which Keith will agree with, or dismiss. It's like pushing lots of buttons, most of which are broken.

On the subject of Rosalind, Keith mentions that she has an exhibition coming soon.

'How is she?'

Keith is silent. Keith is watching the road.

It's not clear who should speak next.

'She's alright,' Keith eventually says.

'Good.'

'We don't have the same creative cycle,' Keith says, as if everyone has a creative cycle.

You can tell that Keith wants to say something more, but doesn't have the words.

Keith turns up the volume.

The music is loud, which means they don't have to talk.

Keith is tapping his finger. 'How long are you staying for?'

'Not long.'

'It's probably better you're here.'

'Why?'

There is silence between them.

You wonder what Keith must be thinking.

Keith looks at the road. 'It doesn't matter.'

'What is it?'

'Nothing,' Keith says. 'You know what women are like.'

'What do you mean?'

Keith looks over his shoulder at the blindspot. 'It's been tense.'

Then, after a pause, Keith says he's hardly spoken to Rosalind this week. It's a shame, Keith says.

'Have you talked about it?'

'No,' Keith says. 'We don't talk much. We took a break for a while.'

'Oh.'

What's the best thing to say?

There is not much time until they arrive. The Royal Free Hospital is signposted on the left.

Then he feels like he ought to say something about love. Go on, Joe. What do you know about love?

'It's like the World Cup.'

'What?'

'A relationship is like the World Cup. If you get knocked out in the final, you might as well have never bothered.'

'I don't watch football.'

'You're at the semi-final stage. You don't want to lose a penalty shootout.'

'Right.'

'You want to stay together and have kids. Like, Brazil.'

Keith sighs. 'I feel like England.'

Five

The main guest room is at the top of the house. You could describe it as an artist's attic. There is a mahogany dressing table and chair. An oval shaped mirror. Some fashion magazines. It has a small balcony from which you can see the rooftops of Hampstead. From the balcony he can see that for once, there is sunshine, and the world seems to match his mood.

Then, at about eleven o'clock, his mobile phone rings on the desk.

'Hello?'

'Just to confirm, do you know Rowan's Bowl?'

'Yeah.'

'We'll meet there at two,' the voice instructs.

It has come about sooner than he thought. Today is the day. He will be free.

It will be a negotiation, as much as anything. When he meets Gideon, there will be plenty of things to discuss.

Will Muriel ever believe him? Probably, but probably will not do.

After the meeting, he will make a plan for the future. He will make time for it, after Gideon. Then he can get away from it all.

*

He walks downstairs, pulls the pink towel from the banister

and enters the bathroom.

Between rising from his bed and walking to the bathroom, he thought for the first time in a while about his nose. If he were younger, the damage would bother him. Now, if anything, he should consider it a blessing.

In the mirror he is reminded of the white cotton strip that conceals the damage. It has managed to remain in position.

For a good ten seconds he looks at his face – the tired, sad eyes – and it strikes him, as he slides his finger down his chin, that he looks exhausted.

What should he say to Gideon? There is plenty to talk about. The most important thing is to get the facts right.

He bends, practising a handshake with thin air.

*

In the kitchen, he has a mug of coffee and the *Guardian* by his side. Although it disappoints him to do so, he reduces his vernacular to what he imagines to be North London casual after Keith asks what he's doing today.

'I need to get my shit together,' he answers.

It disappoints him immediately.

What is he doing today? He must finish the job. There is an order in which he should do these things.

Then he asks Keith if he's alright, which is probably a stupid question.

'Yeah man,' Keith says.

Keith drags on his cigarette and throws it outside.

'I'm really fucking great,' Keith says.

'Good.'

You get the impression that Keith won't be speaking anymore.

Keith slides a knife through an apple and offers him a half.

Keith, in his neck-wrung headphones, scrapes the chair inward and lets him pass. They do not exchange any more words.

*

It's in the high ceilinged studio on the ground floor that Rosalind creates most of her art. The room is reserved exclusively for the purposes of art. Good art, as far as he can tell.

The entire floor is covered in a white sheet. There is nowhere to sit.

A dozen or so canvases lean against the wall. You can see what she's painted. Misshapen women and wilted flowers. On the wall is an art installation made of lacerated posters.

There is a canvas positioned on the easel. The canvas is marked with a couple of blue dots. In pencil, she has drawn an outline of a swan. It might be a clue as to what will become of the canvas. When the painting is given a form, we will probably see the swan.

There is plenty to suggest that Rosalind has been prolific in her work. She is the spirit of the house. She will get on with it, regardless of what's happening with Keith. She will do her best to remain sane, which is about as much as you can hope for. But where is she?

It's here, through the French doors, that he walks outside and meets Rosalind on the patio. For once, she's not in the studio.

She is holding a canister to a washing line, aiming at a pair of stonewashed trousers.

'I didn't know you work out here.'

'I do when the weather's good,' she says.

Today she is wearing a ruffled skirt, and rolled-up cardigan sleeves. She's wearing garden gloves and boots, with a bucket of copper sulphate between her feet.

'You can relax if you want,' she says. 'How's your nose?'

'Good, thanks.'

'Have you called the police?'

'No. I don't want them involved.'

It's difficult to know what to make of the jeans on the

washing line.

For a moment, he wonders whether he is right to assume that the jeans are part of the artwork. Is it just a mad way of doing your laundry? No, it's definitely a work of art.

'What are you working on?'

'I've just come back from Yemen,' she says. 'I'm using sand.'

'Sand?'

'Just a small amount. Could you hold this for me?' she passes a bottle of bleach. She pulls off her gloves and tosses them on the patio. 'I've been quite busy these past few weeks. I've got an exhibition soon.'

She pauses to reflect on the colour of the jeans. The bleach has stained through.

'I'm directing a play as well,' she says. 'I want to perform it in the garden.'

'Maybe I'll come and see it.'

'Maybe.'

A cigarette butt is tossed from the open kitchen and lands beside them.

Rosalind holds the canister forward and lets out a hiss.

He wants to say something. Rather than ask a question, he wants his words to hang in the air.

'Thanks so much for having me.'

She is focused on aiming the canister. 'It's better than hearing you've jumped off a bridge.'

'You must have been surprised when I turned up.'

'Yes,' she says and lowers the canister. 'I suppose it took some sort of balls.'

Then he mentions that he ought to leave. He says that he will return to collect his things.

'I'm going to meet the journalist.'

'Alright.'

'I think it will prove something.'

'To Mum?'

'Yes, and to myself. But yes, to Muriel. I think a part of

her is unsure.'

'Do you blame her?'

There is silence for a moment.

'No, I suppose not.'

'Have you spoken to Mum?' she says.

'She's not answering.'

'Well, that doesn't surprise me.'

When he decides there is nothing left to say, he walks to the kitchen door.

'I don't want to disturb you.'

'No, it's fine. I should take a break anyway.'

'Wish me luck.'

'Okay. Good luck.'

*

When he steps onto the bus later that afternoon, he wants to talk to someone, however strange it seems. He wants to tell every passenger his story and say, wish me luck! It's impossible because most of the passengers are staring away from him. Some of them are wearing headphones. The only thing he misses about the north is that you don't have to make an effort. You never feel underdressed, unlike here, in London, where he can't step outside without feeling old.

It had worried him that people would stare, although it seems that nobody has a clue. His presence appears to register on the face of a mother, who is holding a pram. A woman by the window, about sixty, clearly knows him but can't find the energy to express an opinion. To everyone else, he's just an ageing man dressed as a thirty-something, in his candystripe shirt and smart shoes.

From his position at the window, one row from the back, it's hard to keep still. He taps his finger on his knee, staring at the strip of adverts on the side. One of these reminds him that he needs to book a holiday.

It's about twenty minutes later that the bus steers into the

Finsbury Park terminus and the passengers rise from their seats.

He looks at his watch, stepping off the carriage. One-forty-five.

*

Rowan's Bowl, opposite a traffic island and a railway bridge, is a place that he remembers taking Rosalind to as a child.

On the steps to the entrance, where a lad in a cap is shouting at a security guard, he holds the door and waits for an opening. He passes through the entrance and ignores the man at the counter.

Without having to step any further, he realises that he has been found.

Gideon is there, in front of the arcades.

With his lank hair, Gideon is somewhere on the evolutionary scale between man and horse.

'Hello, Joe.'

What's the best thing to do? It would be weird to shake his hand, but weird, too, just to stand there.

He nods as a form of reply.

'Shall we go somewhere quiet?' Gideon says.

'I don't mind.'

'What do you want to do?'

'I want to talk.'

*

In Finsbury Park there is a railway bridge. It has graffiti and rust and bird shit. He used to come here when Rosalind was about three. She would insist that they wait for the next train to pass and he would stand there, waiting for it to arrive. He would hoist her up and let her watch in silent fascination as the Inter City came underneath. Afterwards she would smile.

'I want to help you, Joe. Don't think that I'm not on your side.'

'Why did you print it?'

'We had a credible source.'

'Who?'

'One of your skeletons, I expect.'

'Do you know who it was?'

'You'll have to ask my editor. I was given the lead. I was assured it was a legitimate source.'

'But it's a lie.'

'As I said, there's nothing to worry about. Margaret and Jim contacted us. They're angry, just like you.'

'So it was a hoax?'

'Probably.'

'Who did it?'

'It was anonymous, as far as I understand.'

It would be a mistake to let his anger reveal itself. This is a performance.

'We wanted to follow it through,' Gideon says. 'Naturally, it's not the sort of thing you brush under the carpet. It seemed legitimate.'

It probably did seem legitimate. We might reasonably believe that having slept with Margaret, and destroyed his own marriage, Helen might be his daughter. We might believe that he abandoned Helen, as the article suggested, and refused to acknowledge her, or provide financial support. It makes a good story that someone who devoted a life to helping the less fortunate could let himself down when it came to his alleged flesh and blood.

You can tell that Gideon is thinking about which words to choose.

'We won't be pushing the story any further.'

'I should think not.'

'Is that enough?'

'No,' he says, and explains that he was hoping for an apology.

Although he can feel the strength in his voice, it's not enough to alter the situation. It requires something more.

'I want you to help me.'

'What can I do?'

'Find out the source.'

'Would it make you happy?'

'It might save my marriage.'

It's a mistake to permit the silence. In the silence Gideon can change his mind.

'I could speak to my editor,' Gideon says.

'And I want a correction. You don't have to apologise. Just correct the story.'

'What do we get?'

'I'll give you a quote. And I won't take any action.'

It seems like a reasonable proposal.

Then he finds himself almost pleading. He wonders how it came to this. He was supposed to be the victim.

'Okay,' Gideon says. 'We'll do a counter story, with quotes from you and Margaret.'

'That's fine.'

'And I'll speak to my editor and let you know what happens.'

'Thank you.'

The bridge begins to shudder.

It's too loud to speak when the train passes beneath. The sound continues to reverberate.

The train has passed.

*

He could walk the whole way home if he wanted. The adrenalin is enough.

As he walks towards the Finsbury Park terminus, in the bright afternoon, he wants his thoughts to converge on a single emotion. He is pleased. Of course, he is pleased. He stuck to the plan and it worked. He came to London to get rid of the lie, and now it's all happening. The plan is coming together. But it doesn't seem real yet. It doesn't seem possible that all this could be over.

And just now, walking amid the pedestrians, in and out of the traffic, it's true that nothing seems of any importance.

Then he wonders if he will ever meet Helen. It probably won't make a difference. She can remain a stranger, in the background somewhere. There is no point in thinking about it any longer.

The result, of course, is the important thing. He got what he came for, didn't he?

With any luck, things will begin to change. There is no need to worry about the future. Everything will work itself out. Things will fall into position. The stars will align, just like they're meant to. He might be able to return north, in the house he had just gotten used to, with his things in their usual place.

Then his thoughts turn to Barry, and he wonders what Barry would have made of it all.

Joe Street, former education secretary. The fallen minister. The lost politician!

A crowd of people are standing at the bus stop. In an ideal world, these people would applaud his arrival.

It only takes a minute for the bus to arrive.

He doesn't mind waiting at the back of the queue.

When he steps onto the bus, he chooses to sit downstairs.

It's a relief when he sits down, because now he can breathe out.

He allows himself to smile.

He has earned the right to smile.

It seems strange that people's faces should not match his own elation. They will be wondering what's making him smile. Let them wonder. If they knew where he'd come from, they'd probably smile too. In fact, they might shake his hand.

He wants to tell somebody his story. The woman at the window might be interested. He leans forward in his seat. He can almost smell the back of her neck. Then he decides that he ought to say nothing. He had better leave her alone.

In a short while he will return to Hampstead. It will be nice to see Rosalind at the door. They will discuss what happened. She might even give him a hug.

Should he buy a bottle of something? Just to celebrate, and say thank you. Yes, he will buy something.

*

In Hampstead he enters a newsagent and picks out a bottle of red wine.

He has the courage to say, 'how are you?' to the man at the counter, whose response is of feigned recognition.

Then he walks down Hampstead High Street with a bottle of wine in a blue plastic bag.

*

For whatever reason, he thought Rosalind would be standing on the doorstep.

He presses the bell because he doesn't have a key.

There is no answer.

He peers through the front window.

There is no-one in the living room.

At the side of the house is the open gate, which leads him to the patio.

On the line is the pair of half-painted stonewashed jeans.

The door to the kitchen is open. He steps into the kitchen.

'Hello?'

He pulls the bottle of wine from the bag and puts it on the table.

He empties his pockets, lifting out some receipts.

It's important to make the phone call.

He lifts the receiver and dials for Muriel.

The phone rings, and he can imagine Muriel sitting in bed, looking at the walls.

Then he is introduced to the answering machine.

There is no point in leaving a message.

She hasn't phoned all week. It'll change when she sees the truth. For now he must wait.

*

'Hello?' he calls again, moving upstairs.

It's reasonable to assume that Rosalind is at the top of the house. She would have answered him, if she were downstairs.

It's a surprise, then, to open her bedroom door and find no-one.

The silence, at least, will give him the chance to think about where to go.

If he wanted, he could probably stay for a couple more nights. It would be uncomfortable for everyone, but what's the alternative? Go home, perhaps.

There is no point going home.

The sensible thing would be to get away somewhere. Six months in a cottage or something. He could discover a village that sounds twee and live there, in a false version of reality. He would like to explore the countryside, but not the sea. The sea did him no good at all.

Sure, he could return to Muriel, but what would that achieve? She will hate him until she learns the truth. When the apology comes, what will he do?

And then he hears a bang from below. Someone is shouting. He steps onto the landing to listen. Did he imagine it? It's not in his instinct to shout, but he leans over the banister.

'Hello?' he calls.

There is a loud shudder as the front door slams.

He walks down the staircase; he doesn't know what to expect.

The house is silent, just as before.

When he enters the studio, Rosalind is standing in the middle of the room.

She is alone.

She is two metres or so from the canvas. She is looking at her work. It doesn't appear to make an impression on her.

To his mind, she looks ill. She looks ill compared to this morning.

'I heard something.'

Rosalind is looking at her painting. It's not clear what she's thinking.

'It was nothing,' she says.

'Where's Keith?'

'I don't know,' Rosalind says with her eyes on the canvas.

For now he should step away. It would be better to say nothing. He can see that.

It's only when Rosalind turns from the painting, and looks at him, that he can see the tear running down her cheek.

'What's wrong?'

She moves closer to him.

Then he is silenced by his daughter, who begins to sob into his shoulder.

He doesn't say anything more, finding to his surprise that he can't speak.

It's easier now to think of her as the girl he once knew. The daughter he held at the railway bridge.

Six

In the plan, this was the day when he would start a new life. He should be looking at a map. He was supposed to be on his way to somewhere. Somewhere in the distance.

He wonders, at this precise moment, what he is doing here.

The plan must change. It's not working in the order he expected. What was the plan again? It was to clear his name and get away from it all. It has become more complicated.

Where can he go now? He wants a cup of tea but is cautious about leaving his room.

The house is somewhere he shouldn't be.

*

When he reads a book the same morning, turning pages without much thought for the words, he can only think about Rosalind. She needs him. It's remarkable to think that she actually needs him.

He flicks the kettle and looks around for something to do.

He will make her something. He can make lunch or a cup of tea. Tea would be better. Tea can solve it.

There is some bread on the counter. He can make tea and toast.

The bottle of wine is on the table. They had better drink it another time.

Her clothes on the floor probably need to go in the wash. He kneels and gathers some, making an effort to ignore the bras and knickers.

Then he waits.

*

He nudges the bedroom door with his shoulder.

Because of the tray, which he carried upstairs with some difficulty, he must enter without knocking.

In truth, the bedroom says nothing about her. It has plain white walls, a large set of windows, an en-suite shower and a wooden wardrobe. It's the kind of room you would expect in a small hotel, pruned of its personality so that it might appeal to everyone. You half-expect to see complimentary chocolates on the pillows. Quite how she has managed to make it so boring is impossible to understand. Even the attic, which is the reject room, has more personality.

It's important to tread with care in order to avoid the scrunched up balls of tissue.

The one good decision was to send her to bed. Get some sleep, he told her. She agreed in so far as she went to the bedroom. The failure, though, is that she is still awake.

She is lying in bed with her face pressed against the pillow.

It's only when he puts the tray on the side that she finds the energy to turn around.

'Thank you,' she can just about mutter.

It's hard to imagine that she'll ever leave the bedroom.

And also, the crying has made her skin look worse. She has exhausted herself just from crying.

Then he puts his hand on her forehead. It seems like the right thing to do.

'If you want to talk... '

'Not now,' she says, her voice holding together.

'Alright.'

It's a shame that Muriel isn't here. Muriel would do better. He can manage tea and toast, but everything else is above his pay grade, as they say.

He puts the door back as it was.

*

He might as well get out of the house.

There is a shopping list on the hall table. He can go and buy her something. He will buy her some stuff and it will give her the space to create things.

He pockets a set of keys from the table.

What can he buy her?

He leans over and writes *mackerel*, *rice* and *lentils*.

He opens the front garden gate and walks in the direction of the high street.

There is about ten items on the list: some things she wanted, some things she might enjoy. There was a magazine called *Aesthetica* in her room. She might like another copy.

Hampstead will probably look the same in ten years.

You know it's an expensive neighbourhood because most of the houses are made of brick and wood.

When you think of its essence, you think of a white chain link fence. If not, you think of those crepe sellers, or the kite-fliers on Parliament Hill. In the distance you can see the tall, dumb towers of the City.

On the subject of money, Rosalind has a lot to think about. How will she afford to keep the house? It would be a good idea to have some sort of income. Without wanting to think about his daughter's mortgage, there is an urgent need for Rosalind to make some money. Keith might want to sell, but she has no money to buy his share. She is not well attuned to the process of making money.

She is doomed, then. Life is an expensive business. You can visit the pubs of Keats and Byron, but it will cost you.

*

In Hampstead, there is a fundamental imbalance between the

number of delicatessens and the number of places you could purchase, say, a hammer.

In the delicatessen, he fills the basket with things she might like.

He runs his finger down the list.

Mackerel.

Rice.

Lentils.

From the refrigerator he lifts a carton of soya milk.

Where is the rice?

He reaches for a pack of rice.

If he wanted to start a conversation with the shopkeeper, he'd say something about organic food. Those words would seem to match the man's appearance. If this sounds judgemental, you would have to judge for yourself. The tweed jacket and white beard shaped his judgement.

The shopkeeper looks at him and says, 'Mr. Street.'

He almost wants to point at himself and say, 'who me?'

It's not a surprise, really. It's not a surprise that the shopkeeper should know his name.

There is a momentary panic when he wonders whether he should know the shopkeeper. No, he would remember if they had met.

The shopkeeper is looking at him as if there is something urgent to talk about.

'Unbelievable, isn't it?'

It takes a moment to figure out what exactly is unbelievable.

Then it becomes clear.

The shopkeeper talks about the prospect of war.

It's unnerving to know that people in Hampstead have worries too. Not worries in the bill paying sense, but worries of a global kind. How disappointing.

If people in Hampstead aren't happy, then who is? Shouldn't it be enough just to have crepes and kites and chinos?

'You were one of the better ones,' the shopkeeper says, lifting the carton into the bag.

'I don't know.'

'We need people like you.'

Then, as always with these conversations, they have discussed the problem and now it's time for a solution.

'You ought to get down there, outside Parliament, with a megaphone, telling it how it is.'

'I should do.'

'Go on then.'

The shopkeeper is right in the sense that he ought to do something – we all should – but what is there to do? If megaphones changed anything, they wouldn't let you use them.

'Do something,' the shopkeeper says.

'Okay.'

'Do you promise?'

'I promise.'

'Excellent.'

Then he collects the bag and moves towards the door.

When he pushes the door and steps onto the pavement, in the sleepy Hampstead afternoon, he feels confident that he can delete the conversation from his mind.

*

On his return, he opens the door and finds the house exactly as it was.

Then he wonders if he is supposed to be here at all. Is he supposed to just disappear?

All he can do is lay the food on the kitchen table.

From what he can tell, Rosalind is still the same. She has probably been lying face down on the pillow for most of the morning, sometimes rising to check her phone on the windowsill. She might not come down. What else can he do? He can bring her things, of course, but what else? What does bringing her things achieve anyway?

He pulls open the fridge. The milk is stale.

Then he pulls out a chair at the table.

He is sitting in front of the red wine, which would be nice to drink, when the occasion allows. He will drink it with Rosalind when she's feeling better. It would be wrong to drink it now.

*

Everything is quiet in the house. Even in the living room with the television on, there is a sense that everything must be quiet.

The studio has been left alone. There are sketchbooks on the carpet. On the shelf are tins that look like varnish pots.

The blue dots on the canvas haven't changed since yesterday. The picture might reflect her sadness; it might reflect nothing. It's hard to make out the swan in much detail. It might be that Rosalind will add more detail when she gets round to it.

Will she ever finish it?

She wouldn't be happy with the picture. She wouldn't want people to see it like this.

*

It's not until the evening that Rosalind acknowledges him. She is there, coming into the kitchen, wearing a hooded jumper and grey pyjama bottoms. It's hard to guess what she's thinking. Is she looking thinner already, or is it his imagination? Could you always see the hipbone above the drawstring?

When she sees the pitta bread on the table it's as though she wants to express her gratitude, but doesn't have the strength. Thanking him would be wrong. It's better to show no emotion.

She has done well just to make it to the kitchen. Food, and the necessity of eating, was what brought her downstairs. If it were possible, she would have stayed in bed all day. Her body demanded that she get something to eat. Maybe she will feel better when she eats something.

She peers into the brown paper bag and, from what he can tell, is happy about what she sees.

'Eat something,' he says, lifting out some salad with a pair of tongs.

You can assume she is beyond the anger stage. She is feeling something else. The word is apathy, or disregard. She wouldn't seem to care if she was dead.

She pours a glass of soya milk.

Then she sits down opposite him.

'I want to burn some things.'

He is silent, which is better than speaking. What are you supposed to say? There is nothing to say, except some kind of blind reassurance.

'You'll be alright.'

'I want to build a bonfire, this evening.'

'Why?'

Her forehead is pressed against the table. 'I want to burn some things.'

If you were to rank the worst candidates for dealing with this, he would rank at number one. The truth is that he can only help in practical ways. It's the emotional part that's difficult.

'Can you start a fire?' she says.

'What are you gonna burn?'

'Some letters. Some of my art.'

'You can't do that.'

'I want to.'

The best he can hope for is to delay the burning. They could watch a film, instead.

'When's your exhibition?'

'I'm not doing it,' she says.

'What do you mean?'

'I'm burning everything.'

'What do you mean, 'everything'?'

'The paintings.'

'But they're amazing!'

Somehow, he should make a sentence about his fondness for the paintings.

There is a painting of a swan, isn't there? It's difficult to make out the swan, but the waves are there, in a line of blue. It's hard to describe the picture without sounding like a weather forecaster.

'I like the one you're doing of the swan.'

'It's shit.'

She mentions how she wants to burn the painting of the swan.

All he can do is persevere.

'Well, I think it's great. It will be, when it's finished.'

'I'm burning it.'

'You should finish it.'

'No.'

'But you must finish it, Ros.'

'I can't.'

'I'll help you,' he says, which only sounds absurd after the words have left his mouth.

'Please just burn it,' she says, drawing out the words as a sort of sigh.

*

From the cellar he pulls out a bag of wood. Some old newspapers. Something to burn.

He gets a chair from the patio and carries it down to the garden.

He loads the wood onto the hollow barbeque grill.

He tears the pack of firelighters.

With his right hand he holds down the newspaper and rips with his left.

He puts the wood and the firelighters and the newspaper in a kind of tepee shape. It's looking good now. It's ready to go up in flames, all of it.

'It looks good,' Rosalind says when she arrives.

Rosalind has brought down a plastic recycling box. It contains a see-through bag of photographs, some books and a small picture.

The picture is a lighthouse shrouded in fog. There's a sadness to it that he can't explain.

'You can have this one,' she says, lifting out the canvas. 'As long as I don't have to look at it.'

It takes a few seconds for the paper to catch fire.

*

When night falls, and the last glimmer of sunlight has gone, he pulls on a jumper and, sitting in front of the blaze, stretches out his legs.

From what he remembers, the garden was supposed to be a place where Rosalind would plant things, not the wild and muddy dumping ground it has become.

She is happy to be sitting there, doing almost nothing. She could be reading a book but instead she is doing nothing.

'Burn something you dislike,' she says.

'Something I dislike… '

'Something that has no reason for being here.'

'I've got a newspaper.'

'Burn it.'

'Do you think it will help?'

'Yes, please burn something. It will be a release.'

*

The owls speak in some secret code, hooting from one tree to the next.

In the flames, you can see his face begin to disappear.

For about a second, you can see the headline:

Job Blow for Street.

Rosalind said the fire would make things better.

Without being certain, you can assume, just by the look of her smile, that she likes the fire. It gives her the ability to forget everything. Were it not for the fire, there would be plenty to think about.

He is glad to be here, and glad about the fire. Why don't they burn things more often?

They should get out to the countryside and catch some fish and light a barbeque in a field.

'He fucked someone.'

For whatever reason, it's a surprise just to hear the words.

'Who?'

'Some girl.'

He pokes the fire with a stick. 'Stupid boy.'

He looks at the ground.

He is probably unqualified to pass judgement on Keith. Even so, it would be wrong to stay silent.

'I'm really sorry. You deserve better.'

What else can you say about it?

He decides to say something general.

'One day you'll look back on this and laugh.'

'You have a warped sense of humour.'

His fist buries deeper into his pocket.

What she said was wrong. The fire has solved nothing.

'I think he's a very disappointing human being,' she says.

'Don't take it to heart.'

'How else am I supposed to take it?'

The fire is still burning. The light from the fire is reflected on her face.

The peril, of course, is that Rosalind won't manage on her own. Not until she's making art again.

Underneath her eyes you can see the faint red rings.

It's about two minutes before anything else is said.

'I'm going away this weekend,' she says.

'Where?'

'To see Mum. We're going to Weston-super-Mare.'

Where is he supposed to go? The idea of spending a weekend with his wife and daughter in a kind of misery club is not something he wants to contemplate. It would be wise, as well, to wait until Gideon has published the correction.

On the log, in front of the fire, he is sitting there with no idea of what to do about it all. He knows what he should feel, but he doesn't know what to do.

'What am I going to do?'

'Read a book.'

'The thing is... I can't really go anywhere else.'

'Then you're stuck here.'

He looks at his daughter. 'I suppose I am.'

Part Two

Seven

George enters the kitchen. The fridge has been left open and the pots are piled carelessly on the side.

He is sick of life in this dank place, with its sweating cooks and broken drawers.

It should be a place to relax but instead it's where all his problems collide. The 3am fights… the drug dealers… the calls from the police. Eden House has become, without question, somewhere he would rather not be.

On most days he is consumed with the same feeling. Something between regret and shame.

There is plenty to do, and so little time. He should make a list but he doesn't have the energy.

Who has put away the tables? Who has locked the windows? Of course, the answer is obvious after a moment's thought. Nobody has, because if he didn't do it, nobody would.

In all the rush, there has been no time to sweep the broken glass. The guests have been fighting. He doesn't know what to do about that.

There is so much to do. He doesn't want to think about it.

The worst thing is the exhaustion.

He has made himself so tired that it would take the longest sleep to recover.

The dark circles under his eyes, for instance, are in danger of becoming a permanent feature. He is too young to look so tired.

The exhaustion has taken something from him. Not his

sense of hope, granted, because nothing can take that. It's more his ability to convince others that he isn't losing his mind.

*

On the door to the office he positions a sign. It says,

Quiet! I am sleeping.

It's a windowless room, set like a prison cell. There are pizza boxes on the floor. A cup of tea has gone cold.

On some nights he sleeps on the couch. It's better than finding his way home.

Just opposite is a small television on top of the filing cabinet. Below are some dirty clothes and a games console.

In front of him is a map of the world. Where might he travel next? He went to Cambodia and Vietnam. It was more fun than anything he has experienced since. It costs money, though.

There is a dartboard on the wall, but the darts have been stolen. He could throw something else. A pen? A pen is no good.

From under the desk he pulls out his rucksack.

On the desk is a copy of a script with some pencilled annotations.

And of course, the telephone.

The telephone actually scares him. It always worries him that it might ring.

Ideally, he would shut the telephone in the drawer. But actually, what good would that do? It would just delay his problems for a while longer.

Then it rings!

It rings, and he steps away.

It might be the police.

It might be his mum, asking why he's not home.

It might keep ringing.

There is something he should remember. What was it? There was a message on the answering machine.

Then it rings again, for a fourth or fifth time, and he doesn't know what to do about it.

He reaches across and lifts the receiver.

'Hello?'

*

On the bus home, which crosses the Thames into Barnes, there is enough time to think about it.

What should he tell his parents?

If he were honest, he would say that he wants to quit.

It's true that running a shelter sounds better as a sentence than as an actual bodily experience. It was something he wanted to say about himself, rather than perform as an active participant.

And what will his parents tell him?

They will tell him to get a real job. Just look at your father, Georgie. Your father began with nothing, except a van, some car aerials, and the ability to make a sale. Now look at him. A millionaire. The story has been told so many times. Sometimes the details change. It's an inspiration to anyone who cares about selling car aerials.

There is no immediate pressure to make money.

There is no reason to work, except to entrench his position within the middle class. It doesn't seem like a dream worth having.

Were his teachers lying then, when they said you could achieve anything?

He doesn't mind the lie so much as the disappointment.

His priority, for the most part, was to find a job that sounded like it had a moral purpose. He found nothing.

In essence, he cut a deal with his mum and dad. If he wasn't going to work, he had to do something valuable. He managed to convince his dad to establish Eden House through a private grant. It made sense – in PR terms – for Eden House to be the flagship charity of the business.

The advantage of pursuing a middle-class vanity project is that you can afford to fuck it up.

*

The house is just a short walk from the duck pond. Further along is Barnes Common.

You couldn't imagine a quieter road in London.

Visitors comment on how lovely everything is. When they say lovely, of course, they mean expensive. If everything were lovely, nothing would be expensive.

There is nothing wrong with it, as such. Everything is pleasant.

In Barnes, you could be forgiven for thinking that nothing bad has ever happened. There might have been a murder, let's say, ten years ago, but it would seem incongruous with the duck pond, the river and the common.

Barnes is sleeping.

He has always assumed, just by listening to others, that he is lucky. There is no reason to assume he is unlucky. Young people can't afford to live here, unless they live with their parents.

Then, with his eyes peering through the glass and an ache in his shoulders, he opens the front door.

For twenty-five years he has lived in the house.

He could live somewhere else, but it would require him to pay rent, and gas, and everything else. One day, he will admit defeat. Then he can struggle like the rest of the world. He would just like a bit more time to prepare for defeat.

*

'You look tired, Georgie,' says his mum, who positions a hot water bottle under his duvet.

He is twenty-five, but he might as well be twelve by the way she pulls the duvet over him.

She puts a hand to his forehead.

She is giving a look that says he ought to explain his tiredness.

'I'm fine.'

'I hope so,' she says.

Then she mentions something about a girl.

'I spoke to her at the bus stop. Do you ever speak to her anymore?'

'No.'

'Oh you should, Georgie. She's lovely. Don't you think?'

'She's alright.'

It would be fine to have the conversation, were it not for the obvious fact that she wants to know why he hasn't got a girlfriend. She is not good at disguising these things.

'She asked how you were.'

'And what did you say?'

'I said you were doing well.'

'So you lied, then?'

'I didn't lie. And don't say that. It makes me worry.'

There is a reason why he doesn't tell her things. It's like talking to an undercover journalist. Somehow, his secrets will make the tabloids, or at least the motherly equivalent, which is to share secrets at the dinner table with relatives.

'She's my favourite, anyway,' she says.

He looks up and says, 'You should ask her out, then.'

'I would, if I were your age.'

'And a boy.'

'Yes, that as well.'

She walks towards the door, content that she won't be getting anything more out of him.

Should he mention the meeting? He might as well.

'I'm meeting Joe Street tomorrow.'

'Really?'

He didn't really want to mention it. She was always going to object on moral grounds.

She looks down and says 'hmm', as if it would be ridiculous for anyone to meet Joe Street.

'Rather you than me,' she says.

She walks to the ironing board and pretends she has something to do.

'Ask him what he thinks about the war,' she eventually says.

'He's against it.'

'Good. He's still a bastard though.'

'I wouldn't believe what you read in the papers.'

For the second time, she makes the 'hmm' sound.

'Sometimes I do,' she says.

'They put out a statement.'

'I wouldn't believe what you read in the statement.'

*

Had it not been for Mum, everything would be clearer in his mind. There would be something else to think about at this very moment, as he steps off the northern line carriage at Hampstead.

She spoke about Joe Street as if he's a man to have contempt for. She must have read the newspaper stories and made a decision, somewhere in her subconscious, to never forget it.

What he knows of Street is the sum total of newspaper headlines, interviews and the occasional column. Street was notorious – if he remembers correctly – for saying things that weren't on the autocue. Gaffes, as they call them. It got so bad that he stopped saying things anymore. To see him lately, you wouldn't appreciate the full depth of his intelligence.

If contempt is the right word, he can think of someone else who is far more deserving of it. He is reminded of Barry, who he met the other week. This Barry had been in contact about his client, Mr Street. It had struck him as an audacious proposal, what Barry had suggested. What did Barry want? It was that they should come to the shelter and give Street the opportunity to meet some of the guests. Yes, there would be cameras and journalists, but you'd get something out of it, see? A win-win. But when it happened, there was a strange atmosphere about it all. There were too many idiots in the room.

Among the idiots, there were none more stupid than the vain, contemptible Barry. It was as if Street had decided to put a gorilla in charge of his affairs, which is what made it entertaining from the outset.

Something was wrong. It was sad to watch.

Before the interview was over, Street rose from his chair and quickly left the building.

There followed the pathetic sight of the gorilla making an apology, and trying to change the wording of the answers. The last thing he remembers was the gorilla running after Street.

So whatever Mum says, Joe Street deserves a chance. Even though his name has been impossible to say without registering some kind of disapproval, he knows him, perhaps, to be a good man. You can never be sure, though.

*

When Street opens the door there is a bigger smile on his face than has been seen for a long time. Is there something to smile about?

Street is more relaxed than the other day, although you wouldn't go so far as to say he looks well. You can't look at the nose without feeling pity. The scab is dry, almost as a black crust.

They say hello; they say what a good thing it is to see each other again.

The living room, whilst clean enough, has a musty, lived-in feel, like someone should open the window.

Then he wonders about the dark-haired girl, who passes without saying hello. She walks to the door, in her slippers and dressing gown, without looking at anyone.

Street calls her name, Rosalind, and she turns around.

She doesn't come any closer. She is standing where she is. You can see she is thin, but naturally so.

From the look of her eyes, it's hard to tell whether she has been crying, or yawning. It makes you wonder what might have happened.

And he can also see, more than he first thought, that she is beautiful.

Eight

A vision for the future has come.

He was looking for something and he found it. For a while, he didn't know what it was. This must be it.

The idea came to him as soon as things turned quiet. It all came rather quickly. It was at this silly moment of doing nothing, really. He was at the sink, washing a plate with a sponge, when it came to him. It was so simple! So simple it felt almost wrong.

At the age of fifty-nine – yes, it has taken him until the age of fifty-nine – he is ready to build something. He thought loneliness would make him mad, but look at the results! A vision for the future.

If there is any doubt about the whole idea then it's Rosalind, right now, who can defeat him. Will Rosalind laugh at him? No, she'll agree to it. She doesn't have the heart to laugh anymore.

There was nothing desperate about turning to George. Actually, it was very desperate. But you can still be a desperate genius.

Whether or not George was born with a silver spoon in his mouth is beside the point. The boy has manners and ambition. If you meet such a person, the best thing is to grab them and never let go.

In the living room, George is sitting exactly where he was before, which strikes him as an obedient thing to do. Why not walk around or look at the photographs? George has done none of that.

Look at George. Look at the pink linen trousers. What would Barry say? On the checklist, the trousers would receive a tick. The mop of hair, though, would get a cross.

Rosalind is silent when she re-enters the living room.

Her sunglasses are resting on her head.

She is staring at the mirror. She's not going to turn around unless spoken to.

'Do you want to hear my plan?'

She looks at her father and has nothing to say. If you could translate the expression into words, it would say something like, 'what are you so chirpy about?'

She smiles at George to acknowledge his presence, but you feel that will probably be the last of it. She won't say anything more than she has to.

'I'm going in a minute,' she says.

'I'll be quick.'

'Go on.'

How should he say it?

'I've got a proposal for both of you.'

It sounds like an arranged marriage. Rosalind, unable to suppress a smile, is thinking the same.

It's important to mention George, his background, and the logic behind inviting him here.

'I think the two of you can work together.'

It's unfortunate that George, at this moment, has the look of a lost child.

There is nothing left to explain, besides the plan itself. The task is to find the right words.

'This place could be perfect as a guesthouse.'

Rosalind is silent.

'We've got plenty of rooms. A garden.'

'What am I then, a maid?'

'You're the artist. The artist-in-residence.'

'What does that mean?'

'You can paint the walls or something.'

Rosalind is waiting. If she liked the idea, she would say something. It's like she's trying to recollect all the many different ways of saying 'no'.

Is she going to speak?

Instead, she holds her mouth and lets out a laugh.

She is laughing, and she can't even look at him.

So that must be it.

How does the idea sound now? It seems stupider than it did just a moment ago. The idea was there and he told her about it. She laughed.

Even George, who has been listening, has nothing to say.

'Is this a joke?' Rosalind says.

'No.'

'Really?'

'It means you can keep the house and carry on as you are.'

'In a guesthouse?'

'It won't be like an ordinary guesthouse. It'll be a collective.'

'A commune.'

'Something like that. We can do something for the homeless.'

'The homeless?'

'We'll employ them. George can help.'

She turns to face George, which is the polite thing to do. The trouble for Rosalind is that she can't laugh at George. As much as she would like to, she has a duty not to laugh.

'What do you think of this?'

'It sounds interesting,' George says. 'I work with a lot of homeless people. Some of them would benefit from skills training. But everyone's different. Don't think of them as all the same.'

George mentions how each homeless person has a story. Eden House, his father's shelter, could provide a number of homeless people with no shortage of stories.

Then George mentions his father, who, by the sound of it, is like a monster that vomits cash.

'It might be good PR for his business,' George says.

Rosalind is silent.

You can't really gauge much from her expression. She is processing all the information in her head.

She has obviously been thinking about it, because she then turns to her father.

'What would you call it?'

'Bevan House.'

'Why?'

'After Nye Bevan.'

'Who?'

'He founded the National Health Service.'

'Bevan Breakfast,' Rosalind says.

There is a receipt on the table.

He writes *Bevan Breakfast*, out of some desire to reach out to Rosalind and her people.

'What exactly will it be?' she says.

'A kind of hotel.'

'I liked how you described it before. You could make it an artists co-operative.'

'What does that mean?'

'We could have a studio that we invite artists to use. An open house.'

'Sure.'

'We could promote the artists.'

'Yes, that could be part of it.'

'It will be a not-for-profit, right?'

'Yes.'

'But we use the rates to cover the mortgage?'

'Yes, we share the money.'

'And the profit?'

'We can employ the homeless. It'll be a cycle.'

There is a big moment coming. If he can find the words, she might agree to it all.

'The most important thing is that we devote our time to something bigger than ourselves. I want to build something we can feel a part of.'

'As long as you don't fuck it up.'

There. That's probably all she has to say.

Is she satisfied? She is smiling. It doesn't mean she is satisfied. She might not want to live in a guesthouse. She might have other plans.

She lifts the bag over her shoulder. 'I'll say goodbye now as I'm going in a minute,' she says.

'How does it sound to you?'

'I have no problem with it,' she says. 'If it doesn't work, it doesn't work. I don't even care anymore.'

'Would you rather rent it out?'

'No. I couldn't live with strangers.'

'What about the guests?'

'I don't plan on speaking to them.'

George, who has been listening, looks at Rosalind in a way that makes you think of patience.

'I'd be happy to help,' George says. 'Joe and I could do the ugly stuff.'

There is a list of ugly things.

The drainpipe. The toilet. Something else.

The homeless, too, will do lots of ugly stuff.

Not everything will be ugly, though.

There will be music.

And artwork.

The guesthouse will be a triumph.

The advantage, George says, is that people will recognise Joe. It will be a sensation.

'I think we can do it,' George says. 'This could be big.'

Does Rosalind know what to say?

It wasn't a question, what George said. Still, it requires an answer.

'Maybe,' Rosalind says.

Then she mentions her artwork, and how it hasn't really happened of late.

'I need to take a break from it,' she says.

George smiles. 'Are you an artist?'

She smiles at the question. She must be the only person who can smile without looking happy.

'Sometimes,' she says, gesturing with her hand towards the studio.

George peers into the studio and she follows him inside.

Is there any point in following them?

The conversation will have an obvious pattern. George will mention how amazing the paintings are. Rosalind, rather than take it as a compliment, will say no, it's all shit. She will deflect attention from herself. This is her thing.

From the hall you can hear them talking.

The words don't make any sense. They might as well be speaking another language.

Where does he go?

It's an unspoken code that the three of them wouldn't be able to sustain a conversation about art. To speak about it would be a mistake. The ideas are beyond his critical understanding. That's the reasoning, and he hasn't decided whether to resent it.

When they return, they are speaking in the middle of a sentence.

What did Rosalind say that made George smile? She said something. She said she has a bad case of papillon noir. What is that?

You get the sense that, for his benefit, they won't speak about art anymore.

Rosalind moves closer. 'I'm going. I'll tell Mum about your crazy plan.'

'Do you think she'll mind?'

'She won't care.'

'When is she coming to visit?'

'Never. She knows you're here.'

It's only when the words have left her mouth that she appears to realise what she's said. She puts a hand on his shoulder. 'I'll ask her. Maybe she'll come.'

Then Rosalind walks to the front door.

She looks at George and says it was nice to meet him. They agree to share something – something to do with his writing? – once she has returned. Will she ever return at all? You would have to assume so.

'I'll print you a copy,' George says.

'Please do.'

George, by the look of his face, is excited by the prospect. It's like no-one has ever asked to read his work.

Rosalind opens the front door. She doesn't make a fuss when she exits.

George pulls on his coat and says he will speak to his dad. 'He can probably help us,' George says.

You can imagine what Barry would say. 'It's alright for some,' or something like that.

Barry would hate George.

Barry would hate the whole thing. This is the best part.

*

It's only by doing nothing, as the hours pass without event, that everything begins to make sense. It didn't make sense until he started doing nothing.

He can look at everything from a distance. If he were to guess, a majority of people would believe the idea has some merit. That's just a guess, though. It's not possible to have an objective view.

He is glad, most of all, that things are beginning to happen.

He can think of the house not for what it is, but for what it might be. A sanctuary. For so long he has wanted a sanctuary. And now, running his finger along the banister, he has something to think about.

The plan must be to build something.

He begins to think of all the possibilities. There are too many to think about all at once.

The house must be viable. It needs to work.

It will be a guesthouse, although not in the conventional sense. It must attract a certain kind of spirit.

The staff will offer more than slavish duties. The whole ethos of the place will be to live as a community. Community is important.

The guests will be expected to share.

There will be books on the hall table.

The life of the house will come from its people. It will be alive in friendship, laughter and song.

On Bonfire Night, they will stand on the balcony, looking at all the fireworks.

Everyone will be treated with respect.

It will be an experiment on how to live. It will be a very sophisticated zoo.

They will build something real, something you can cling to.

People will visit from every part of the world. It will be society's triumph, and he won't apologise for the arrogance in this thought. He can decide what triumph looks like.

You could call it a dream.

As a boy, he had the same excitement as he feels now. How might he shape the world? This is how. It took fifty-odd years to rediscover the spirit of the boy.

This is the dream.

Cruelty has ruled for too long. We have forgotten about kindness. Let it be our turn.

Nine

Look at the house.

It has history, no doubt. You can make a virtue of history. People want something real, something they can belong to. They want the house to have been visited by Byron on his way to Harrow, however much of a lie that may be. They want a plaque at the entrance that tells the name of a famous poet. They want to *do* England, even if it means ignoring England.

If you put a time-lapse camera in the living room it would show that many things have changed. The sofa has been moved against the wall. On the mantelpiece is a vase of flowers.

The hall is crowded with boxes and bubble-wrapped frames. There is a toolbox, some tins of paint and the parts of a wardrobe, which he will attempt to assemble.

The tour has been planned in his head. It's better to do it in the right order.

The order is what? It's the hall, the living room, the kitchen, the bathroom, the first and second bedroom, the view from the skylight and to finish, the view from the balcony.

But perhaps the view is unimportant. George senior would be satisfied if the view was of nothing.

'Don't worry about him,' George says, before the man has even set foot in the house.

George's father – who is also called George – must be worth a million or two.

It feels like an old relative is coming. It's as though he must spend some time in front of the mirror, just to make sure he looks acceptable. He should watch his language, too.

The purpose of the visit is threefold.

Is the project viable? It must be fully costed, and if a grant is forthcoming, the house must reflect well on the sponsor.

Then, George senior will need to establish the relationship between Eden House and Bevan Breakfast. There will need to be a queue of homeless people who would like to learn new skills.

Without even having met George senior, the man sounds like someone who will almost certainly hate him. They will probably disagree about everything. What can they expect to share in common? The mind of a wealthy businessman bears no relation to the mind of a browbeaten socialist. Their mutual fondness for oxygen is about as much as they will share. This might be wrong. George senior might be a radical defender of the proletariat. Maybe they'll laugh at the same jokes. They might agree about everything. All of this is possible, but none of this is likely.

*

Just before two o'clock, he is alerted by the sound of the doorbell.

The younger George, in his striped jumper, says, 'Come in, Dad.'

So this is George's father, then. A man who appears to be enjoying the pipe and slippers stage of life.

George senior is older than he expected. Imagine a seventy-year-old in a baseball cap, with a jumper tied around the waist. Glasses, too. The man doesn't dress very well, although you suspect that if he wanted to, it would be possible. There must be some kind of comfort to be had in a white golf shirt. It gives the impression of minimal effort. It's just about enough.

The two Georges look like father and son. You wonder whether they have anything else in common.

George senior says, 'Afternoon Mr. Street,' in what you

assume is an ironic, rather than deferent, tone.

It would be strange if someone really called him Mr. Street. It's an old-fashioned thing. It's not a bad thing, as such. It's just that courtesy, and formal manners, do not belong in this house.

'Afternoon, George.'

There is a handshake.

'Welcome to Bevan Breakfast.'

There is no smile. It's not that George senior is rude. You get a sense that he'll smile on his own terms. As of yet, there is nothing to smile about.

They move into the living room, which is the cleanest room in the house.

George senior will appreciate the tradition of the house, but not so much the people inside it.

George senior positions himself on the armchair. 'You've been in the news, haven't you?'

'That's right.'

'Poor little girl.'

'She wouldn't want to be pitied.'

'Am I right in assuming it's been dropped?'

'Yes.'

'They made a correction, didn't they?'

'They did.'

A decent start.

You would hope the worst is over. The hardest question is out of the way. From now on, they can debate the mechanics of the project. His character is not in question. It's good that George senior mentioned it. This way there is a mutual understanding. He's not a risible, immoral bastard. They can agree upon this. And besides, George junior can vouch for him, and Rosalind too. Not Muriel, admittedly. But anyway, two out of three is good enough.

The younger George is sitting by the window. You half expect George to rise from his seat and ask if they'd like a cup of tea.

The conversation could flow naturally if they wanted it to.

Because of the silence, which must have caused some alarm, George mentions something about the gutter press.

'About two-thirds of the tabloid media are not fit for purpose,' his father replies.

George senior says that many tabloid journalists are scurrilous weasels with shit for brains. In different words, admittedly, but the sentiment is the same.

They agree on something, then. What else can they agree about?

The subject moves onto the war. How do you broach the subject? War should be something beyond debate. If you want to kill, you should do your own killing.

Then, as if by some miracle, George senior says he is an opponent of the war. Not for reasons of compassion, of course. It's more of a practical thing. George senior has a list of practical reasons, rather than emotive ones.

'It's the wrong war,' George senior says.

Between the two of them, there follows a string of clichés over the next five minutes.

Regime change.

Chemical weapons.

Exit strategy.

Whatever meaning these words once had has long since disappeared. There is no meaning in any of it.

You get the impression that George senior came with the expectation of having an argument. In this sense, it has been a very disappointing encounter. There is no argument. There is a strange kind of stasis.

To a degree, he can talk as he wishes. Of course, it's not the same as speaking to an urbane university lecturer, let's say. But it's not as bad as it might be.

You can see that George senior is opinionated, but willing, to some extent, to keep his opinions to himself. This is a good thing. Of course, if you were to venture a little further, and mention immigrants, northerners and travellers, then George senior would probably say what he thinks. But on the safe terrain – the stuff in the middle – they are able to manage a peace.

In light of what George warned, he could have been forgiven for thinking that a vampire was coming for lunch. In fact, George and his father are not very different. George senior is engaging, articulate, and, by the sound of it, a literate man. He is the worst kind of conservative.

'Let's talk about your project,' George senior says.

This is the moment when everything will probably go wrong.

It feels like he must give a business pitch. This is a bad idea. After all, he has the financial literacy of the government of Zimbabwe. Let it be said though, that compassion is just as important as bean counting. It's the philosophy that's important. It shouldn't matter about the bricks and mortar. It's the ethos that counts. It's the idea behind it, rather than the bricks. He can make it work by the force of his desire, rather than his numeracy. Besides, George can do the maths.

'What are your costs?' George senior says.

It's only when he thinks for a moment that it seems quite obvious.

The main expenditure will involve paying Rosalind's share of the mortgage. This is a joint responsibility, which seems fair, considering that Rosalind has given him a room. It's also fair that a homeless member of staff will be paid a nominal wage.

How will they pay for everything? The guestroom rates will be put to this effect. Anything extra will go towards living costs, as well as a proportion of the electricity, water, gas, telephone and tax.

The guests will be encouraged to bring their own food. In return, they can use the house as they wish.

There will be lots of fundraising events, too.

Then he explains to George senior that it will work as a cycle.

'Think of it as an extension of Eden House.'

There is nothing that can be gauged from George senior's expression. It might be a rule of business. Don't lay your cards on the table.

The pitch went well. He said everything that was necessary.

'As a PR proposition, I think it's sound. I expect your involvement should give it some legs.'

What else?

'I'd like it to be self-financing,' George senior says. 'But I'm willing to offer you a small loan. Interest-free.'

When it comes to numbers, it's important to make the decision by committee. If he were to make the decision alone, he would ask for anything between one pound and a million quid.

Between the three of them, they discuss a figure of about five thousand pounds. When the guesthouse begins to grow, the money will be repaid.

George is sitting with a notepad on his lap.

'I'm doing some numbers,' George says.

George tears off a sheet of paper, and, resting on a magazine, presses the nib of the pen on the page.

There are some numbers in black ink.

With George, you have the distinct impression of sharing a room with someone who is thinking all the time. This is something likeable about George. The man has an unshakeable belief in his own ability. It's not arrogance. It's simply the unspoken acknowledgement of his talent as a fact.

'We could run a campaign,' George says. 'We could make some posters.'

There is no reason to quarrel with the idea. He looks at George and says something to the effect of yes, let's do it.

'Now, let me be clear,' George senior says. 'I will take no responsibility for the failure of this project. The moment things turn awry, I'll disassociate myself from it.'

This remark is counterbalanced when George senior then says, 'For my part, I will ensure you get whatever help is necessary.'

At this moment, he has identified the essence of George senior. The man is kind, but only within a rigid definition of kindness specified in a terms and conditions contract. George senior is the sort of man who will doff his cap to a police officer. The most important thing in the world is that everything is working as it should. Listening to George senior makes you think of Titus Salt, who built a tower to watch the workers in his model village.

In the long run, what can George senior do for them?

When the question is raised, George senior has a look that suggests he is still thinking about it.

George senior says they will discuss a grant if, and when, the project is a success.

'First, let's think about Georgie,' George senior says. 'He can help you with recruitment, and advice. He won't cost you a penny, of course. At the moment, Georgie works for free.'

George smiles as if to make light of it all. The smile can be explained quite simply. It's not cool to be a twenty-five-year-old without a paid job. It's not cool to live with your parents. It's not cool, but in London, of course, it's what lots of people do.

'Really, I'd like Georgie to get some more experience,' George senior says. 'But I want him to stay at Eden House, as well. This is a part-time thing.'

George – or is it Georgie? – is nodding his head.

Then George senior says, 'So gentlemen, do we broadly agree?'

There is a collective 'yeah,' in which you can detect a hint of faux-surprise.

Then you get the usual stuff.

It was good to see you, gentlemen.

I look forward to seeing you again.

All of that. The usual.

The two Georges speak for a moment about some family engagement.

The front door opens.

George senior waves a solitary hand from the pavement.

That's everything, then.

George is looking at him with a kind of 'how do you think it went?' expression.

'It went well.'

'Yes, I thought so.'

Everything has been decided.

They agree, without much being said, that Bevan Breakfast will be a total success.

Ten

In much the same way he dislikes newspapers, he dislikes the television too. He would gladly do without it.

The television is alive in the living room.

The newsreader says that a soldier killed in Afghanistan this morning has been named by the Ministry of Defence.

All he can glean from the newsreader is that war is inevitable. It seems that everyone has an opinion and they want to do something about it. What is there to do? According to the news, there is a march scheduled for the weekend. He ought to go. Will it make a difference? No, but he still ought to go.

Unfortunately, there will be lots of people on the march that he doesn't want to see. Muriel will be there. She is yet to digest the news of his innocence.

However much he ought to do something, he shouldn't trouble himself with the war. Let the politicians deal with it.

What would he say to the marchers? He is too disengaged to make an argument. If he wanted to talk about corrupt kings and cheating ministers, it would all relate to a twentieth century world. It would somehow seem like old news.

There is a sense of guilt, undeniably. It took George senior to bring the war to his attention again. That's what happened. Had George senior not mentioned it, he might have forgotten the war completely.

Of course, he never used to be so ignorant.

On the opposition benches he would shout things at his opponents.

In the pub, he would drink and talk until everyone agreed with his opinions. He would have loud discussions about the problem of objective truth.

Sometimes at night he would walk down the steps at Westminster Bridge. There are less people there than you would expect. There is nothing to do unless you like to look at things. On the water is the golden reflection of the Houses of Parliament. Just opposite is the London Eye and the curve of County Hall. It's a pleasure to stand there, a pleasure to be alive and connected to something. That's how it feels when you're standing by the Thames at midnight. You can never own London, but you can belong to it. It's impossible to dominate, but you can dip in and out of it, finding whichever small piece you wish to possess.

*

Rosalind is going to return. She said she would return approximately now. There are so many things to do that he had almost forgotten Rosalind would return.

This will be the start of it. Co-ordination. How can he co-ordinate? Everyone in the house will be busy. Everyone will do something.

The plan is to give it a week before opening. That way they can finish the things that need to get done. They can mend the bathroom door and clear out the cellar. Sell some junk.

When the house is ready, he will think of it as a home. Muriel might also want to live here. This is a conversation they ought to have.

In terms of his public image, it will be a recovery. It will be a chance to show Muriel who he really is. She might fall in love with him again.

*

'I'll carry this,' George says in the kitchen, lifting a green plastic box. 'Where shall I take it?'

'To the cellar, please.'

George, to his credit, is always lifting things. It would be wrong to expect George to lift things all the time. George is a thinking man. Look at his t-shirt. It has a logo supporting the presidential campaign of Michael Dukakis in 1988.

George is nudging the cellar door with the box in his hands.

Most of their conversations occur in one-minute spasms between lifting things.

They talk for a moment about where they might want to put the sign. The front lawn would be a good spot. They will ask Rosalind to make the sign.

'I've spoken to a solicitor about the name Bevan Breakfast,' George says. 'It's absolutely fine.'

'Good.'

'And I've spoken to a couple of investors. I don't suppose you've thought about outside involvement?'

'No, this is our baby.'

Is he averse to money? Not necessarily. Take the example of George senior, for instance. It's more the case that he wants to maintain a level of control.

As long as George is around, there should be nothing to worry about.

They agree to launch an email campaign. It's about raising the profile of the project. Bevan Breakfast is opening.

The final thing is that George has invited a lad from the shelter this afternoon.

'You'll like him,' George says.

There is nothing left to talk about, other than to say how exciting everything is.

'I can't wait,' George says.

'Me neither.'

'Have you thought about inviting your wife?'

'No.'

At the thought of seeing Muriel, he doesn't want to talk anymore.

*

In the attic he has felt a kind of guilty peace. It's the most peaceful room in the house, which is what makes it a privilege to be here. It could have been another way. It could have been worse. Luck has been available to him these past few days. It was never available until he came to Hampstead.

He can only just hear the footsteps in the hall. The sound of the front door closing is a bit more pronounced.

A part of him still expects to hear Rosalind say, 'I'm home!'

Of course, he ought to know better. They will speak to one another when they happen to be in the same room. Not before.

On the way down to the hall you can hear the television in the living room.

The door to the studio is closed. The room, where Rosalind used to spend more time than anywhere else, has become somewhere estranged. It has been spared any makeover, in favour of polite neglect. It has been allowed to remain as it always was. There will be forgotten items – things like matchboxes and inkpots – on the table. It must still contain the easel with the canvas. There will be varnish pots on the desk. Her photo albums will be laid on the side. The canvas will probably have the same line of blue. Nothing will have changed.

She didn't announce that she was home. She entered the hall, and like with everything else, she didn't make a fuss of it. She just opened the door and went into the living room. Is she angry?

It makes him think about all the things she might have said to Muriel.

They might have spoken about the guesthouse. Muriel might have given it her endorsement. Muriel might come and visit!

When he imagines the things that Muriel must be up to, it must be the same as Rosalind, whose art comes third, behind idleness and despair.

They somehow manage to avoid looking at each other until he is sitting down.

Rosalind is just as she was, albeit smiling a little more. Is she smiling? It might be something he has imagined, of course.

It's only in moments such as this that you can see what damage has been done.

Then he says 'how was she?' under the assumption that both of them know who 'she' is.

It's not in her nature to do small talk, although what's in her nature is impossible to know.

'Fine.'

'Does she hate me?'

'I think she's too busy to hate you.'

'Has she seen the correction?'

'Yes.'

'And?'

'She said, 'oh, good'.'

'And that was it?'

'Yes.'

'Did she say anything else?'

'No.'

'What did you talk about?'

'We talked about me, believe it or not.'

'What did she say?'

'She thinks I should focus on my work.'

In fact, Rosalind mentions that Muriel is in favour of the guesthouse.

Muriel said something like, 'It will give you the freedom to express yourself, Ros.'

Then Rosalind pulls something from her bag.

She lifts a sheet of paper on which she has drawn something. It's a rose entwined in a cloud. Underneath, it says Bevan Breakfast.

'There's not a lot to do in Weston-super-Mare.'

It's nice to know that she has done something. What else might she do?

'I'm going to paint something.'

'What for?'

'The walls.'

She takes off her black cardigan. She is holding a hairgrip with her teeth.

'We need to make use of the light,' she says. 'I'll give each room a different theme. And I'll shift some things around.'

'That's great. I'm really glad.'

'I've thought about making you the centrepiece.'

'Me?'

'Your face.'

It must be Rosalind's way of saying sorry for something. Sorry for what? She doubted him. She thought it might be true. She thought he was a liar. She'll still hate him for Margaret, of course. But she was wrong to hate him for Helen.

He can feel himself getting tired and in the mood to say something stupid.

His mind turns to the problem of Muriel.

'When is she coming here?'

'I don't think she is.'

'I thought she would make a bigger fuss.'

'Like what?'

'I don't know.'

'She said she was pleased for you. But we talked about me, most of all.'

'And do you feel better?'

'I do.'

Rosalind is smiling.

He is glad that she is smiling.

*

The kitchen has become somewhere you might actually want to sit. It has plenty of space to relax. You can imagine the room full of strangers, all of them talking among themselves, and forgetting about the war.

'I'd like you to meet a friend of mine,' George says. 'Daryl's done really well so I thought I'd put him on to you.'

George and the lad are sitting at the kitchen table.

Daryl is small and similar in appearance to a vole.

It would be condescending to address him like a vole. He should talk as he would to anyone else. Yes, he should be distant and disappointing.

'Has George told you about the project?'

'Yes,' Daryl says. 'Thanks for having me.'

'Not at all.'

You only have to look at Daryl for a minute to understand his crisis. What is it? The boy has no confidence. It's not the sort of shyness that makes him turn red. It's the sort that manifests itself in silence. Daryl would be perfectly happy to sit there and say nothing at all.

Even so, you can tell that he is sweet. Daryl would probably be loyal, were you to appoint him for a job.

There is little to gain from the situation. Nothing will come of the meeting, except the satisfaction of helping the lad. This is what it's all about.

Then he fills the silence with a cough.

Whoever decided that he should lead the conversation was making a mistake.

Everyone wants to listen; no-one wants to talk. If everyone is listening, there will be nothing but silence.

Daryl says, 'Are you a politician?'

'Not anymore.'

'What do you do now?'

'This,' he says, opening the fridge. 'Do you want a beer?'

Daryl smiles. Despite his best efforts, Daryl fails to prevent his teeth from showing.

'Cheers.'

'That's alright.'

There is no need for etiquette.

It makes him feel like a boss in a Victorian workhouse. Please sir, and all that.

He fills the glass with beer. 'You can work for as little or as long as you like. I trust you'll get things done.'

'Okay.'

'But we'll co-ordinate between us. We'll do a burning. We like to burn things.'

George looks at Daryl and says, 'The idea is to help you get a bit of money together. This way, you can find a landlord and move on. Someone else will come in your place. It's like a conveyor belt, you understand.'

'Yes,' the vole says.

Daryl explains what a relief it will be to have some kind of income. What Daryl also needs is a place where he can sometimes sleep. The couch will do.

'I've been sleeping under a bridge,' Daryl says.

'Oh dear.'

'Then someone introduced me to George.'

'Oh, good.'

Then the conversation moves onto football. It's a great leveller, football. It makes everyone depressed. It doesn't matter how rich you are - it ruins your weekend.

Daryl is a supporter of Leyton Orient. Daryl made this revelation as if it were some kind of magnificent fact.

'How about you?'

'I don't have a team. I used to watch Queens Park Rangers, although I can't tell you who plays for them. I took Rosalind once when she was a kid and she hated it. That's the problem when you don't have boys. Do you have a family?'

'I have a baby coming,' Daryl says.

'Congratulations.'

Daryl looks at the floor and says, 'No, not really.'

They should talk about something else.

He can see Rosalind in the garden, pulling socks from the clothesline.

Then she carries a basket into the kitchen. She is wearing

denim jeans and a dotted shirt.

She says she will be joining them in a minute. They hadn't arranged a meeting, but she knows she could join if she wanted.

This is the place where they will meet once a week. It will require them to share the same space. For the rest of the week they can do as they wish.

She pulls out a chair and says hello.

What does Daryl say?

Nothing.

Despite the silence, you can tell that Daryl is engaged. Daryl smiled at the right moment.

She looks at George and says how much she enjoyed reading the script.

George says, oh, thanks.

Rosalind says that she found the ending very powerful. When she says this, she is holding her hand close to her heart. It might be true, then. She must have enjoyed the ending.

'I used to have a season ticket,' Daryl says.

Where have the words come from?

The words have nothing to do with anything.

Then he realises that Daryl is looking at him. The words came from Daryl.

Without wanting to say anything, it seems there are two conversations running parallel. One is about football; one is about art.

'I loved the dialogue,' Rosalind says, looking towards George.

'I used to sit behind the goal,' Daryl says.

Then George says it took him a year to write.

'It's wonderful,' Rosalind says. 'You should perform it in the garden.'

'They moved the away fans,' Daryl says.

'Oh, right.'

'Do you think?' George says.

'I do.'

Daryl says he is losing interest in the top flight.

'It's not a very competitive league.'

Then, in reply to Daryl, he mumbles something about money ruining football.

George says, 'Would you like to direct it?'

'Yeah,' Daryl says. 'It's a joke, really.'

Rosalind smiles and says, 'That'd be amazing!'

Rosalind and George mention some of their friends who could participate. Costume designers. Actors. Make-up artists.

'Let's do it,' George says.

'We should watch a game,' Daryl says.

'Sure.'

'I'm excited.'

'Me too!'

'Great.'

Silence.

The four of them look at one another.

Three of them are smiling. Only three.

Eleven

He can hear laughter. And then the sound of something read aloud. You can tell it's read from a page and not spoken naturally because of the nervousness of the voice. Nobody talks like that.

There is a conversation on the lawn and he is glad to be looking from a distance.

When he looks closer he can see, through the window, a middle-aged man in glasses, viewing a script in the manner of a tourist squinting at a map. An actor. Someone who wishes to act.

George is trying to make an argument by making shapes with his hands. A gesticulation, if that's the word.

Rosalind is silent, although she appears to understand the essence behind whatever George is saying. Is this how you rehearse a play? It's just a series of conversations on the lawn.

George is the writer, and George, this morning at least, was at pains to say how the play wouldn't distract them from everything else.

'It's all part of the same thing,' George said.

What does this mean? The guesthouse is the play; the play is the guesthouse.

If he were to descend the patio steps, and meet them on the lawn, he would have nothing to say. At most, he could offer them a cup of tea. He would have to watch for longer before he could make a judgement. This is the problem.

Let them dance, and sing, and whatever else they do.

He didn't think he would watch for so long. What makes it compelling is the thought of seeing people happy. Something has prompted them to smile. They have made the lawn somewhere worth standing. Before, it was a place to burn things and nothing else.

George is holding a script, looking down on the page.

Rosalind's approach is to walk and read aloud.

They are focused on the art, the thing itself. They invest a lot of energy in words.

It's a modern play. You can tell as much from the language. It's a family drama and everyone seems worried about the mother. There is something wrong. They don't know what to do.

*

The person he has spoken to the most is Daryl. The lad has been kind enough to clean the bathroom, which took a short while.

As a group, they had agreed that Daryl should begin immediately. The more that gets done, the less trouble they will have upon the launch date.

In the kitchen, Daryl is tying the knot of a bin liner.

Daryl says something about a football result.

What Daryl said is unimportant. It was something about an offside goal. That's all you need to know. If football never existed, you wonder what they'd ever talk about.

The moment will come when he must admit to the lie.

What's the lie?

The truth, Daryl, is that I haven't gone to a game in years. That will be it.

As a compromise, Daryl will probably mention the legends of yesteryear. Oh God.

They ought to speak about something else. It won't happen, but it's something they should try. A life without football is a kind of freedom. It's like a life without God.

'What do you want me to do with this?' Daryl says, lifting the swollen bag of rubbish.

An executive decision is required. After some consideration, he instructs Daryl to put the rubbish in the bin outside. It feels wrong to instruct Daryl on these sorts of things. Daryl should do what he wants.

*

The next time Daryl makes himself known is later that afternoon. Daryl is calling aloud. It's a cue for more football, and more misery.

In the hall, Daryl is pointing at something.

Daryl smiles and says, 'Have you seen your face?'

'What do you mean?'

'Come and look.'

It takes a short while to realise what the fuss is about.

In the hall is a canvas. It's a picture that will hang on the wall. It will be one of the first things that guests see upon entering. A picture of his face.

Strangers will see his digitally re-enhanced face on a vomit themed canvas. It has a red and orange background with his face in the middle, in a kind of pixilated composition of paint and words and photographs.

It has an old photograph of him from the 1980s. He is standing outside a terraced house in Hartlepool, looking at the camera, in his tweed jacket, and with a folder under his arm. The old Joe. It looks ridiculous to position such a photograph within its new context - a million pound house in Hampstead. It makes him wonder what the old Joe would have thought of it all. What would the man in the tweed jacket have said?

It's a shame that the one piece of art that depicts him should be so terrible.

What a shame that his face has been reduced to this.

This is how he should be remembered. A bad work of art.

'What do you think?'

Does he need to explain himself? It should be obvious by the fact of his silence.

He is smiling, which is enough. The smile would suggest that he likes the picture, which, of course, is a lie. The colours are too pronounced. If you could pick one word to describe it, something like 'severe' would do.

It doesn't have an effect, except to make him feel embarrassed. If this was the intention, it has been a success.

What else can you say about it?

You can tell what Rosalind is going to do with the tins of paint in the hall. She will make another painting. Of course, she won't just paint something normal. There will be a theme or a message. It will say something about the world.

Just imagine what the house will look like when she has finished.

*

There was something he knew he had forgotten.

There is a march happening, and where will he be?

Far away.

Aside from Daryl, the house will be empty. Daryl has other things to do.

Where is George?

He can see, immediately in fact, as he enters the living room, that George is waiting for something. George is standing with his hands in his coat pocket. The mop of hair is combed neatly to the side.

Rosalind is gathering a camera from the table.

She lifts her bag and asks if he's coming.

There is no reason why he shouldn't go. In his head, there ought to be a reason.

'Is Muriel going?'

'We're meeting her.'

Rosalind walks into the hall.

She is looking at the mirror. She is wearing foundation; she has made an effort for the first time since Keith. You wouldn't say she looks like an activist.

George follows.

George is a polite boy, someone you could introduce to a stranger and feel confident they would have something to talk about.

Rosalind and George are standing in the hall.

What should he do?

Really, he should attend the march. He should be there, doing his bit.

Then he says, 'I should probably stay.'

Rosalind is frowning.

Let her frown. She is right to frown.

There is not enough energy for an argument.

The front door is open.

'See you later,' Rosalind says.

Goodbye.

The door is shut.

They will be marching without him.

'Any transfer news?' says a voice, which, after a quick inspection, belongs to Daryl.

*

A march against a war is happening on his television screen.

Whatever happens in the future, he will not be able to pat himself on the back for having attended the march. He will tell people that he was sitting in the living room, in front of the television, with a feeling of shame.

The images are exactly what you would expect of a march.

Lots of the people are holding whistles to their lips.

There is a line of police officers.

You can see Big Ben above it all.

Somewhere, Muriel will be standing with a sign. He almost wants to sit a safe distance from the television, just in case she's there, in front of the camera lens, with something to say.

He thought he wouldn't go near the television. But he owes it to himself, and whoever else, to watch the news.

The guilt was already here. It's just that now it feels more certain.

What is he feeling? Not much at all.

The war will be a catastrophe, but what does he care?

This is how it happens.

This is the process by which he will become an old, grumpy man. Your morals are crushed. Your sense of right and wrong disappears. You have a secret contempt for people. Why not just hurry the process along and tie him to a drip?

A change has happened. He was once what you would call a man of ideas. He used to spend a lot of time talking about everlasting light bulbs. The story goes that if a scientist invented an everlasting light bulb, companies would lobby to prevent it reaching the market. He used to get angry about light bulbs. Now it bores him.

This is what he has become. No passion. No fire. No guts.

He lifts the remote and presses the button. The screen turns black.

He can pretend that everyone else has no passion, no fire…

Twelve

There is something about the night. It gives him too much time to reflect.

In a perfect world, it would be better to drag the mattress into the garden. He could sleep among the squirrels.

As he lies there, pulling the duvet up to his chin, he is reminded of everything he wants to forget. Barry. Muriel.

Has he ever felt so distant from the woman he's supposed to love?

He would like to make it work, but that means he would have to meet her halfway. Muriel must do the other half.

Somewhere, at the pit of his unconscious, is the fear that everything might go wrong. The guesthouse will fail. Muriel will continue to hate him.

There is no reason why the night should have this effect. Not a valid reason, at least. There will be guests coming soon. What version of himself will he present to them? It remains to be seen.

It's better just to carry on. If you believe in something, you mustn't doubt. Just make it happen.

*

Through the skylight you can see the moon.

Someone is shouting.

And then he can hear it again.

He can hear the shudder of the kitchen door.

Nothing is certain.

There is shouting down below. Someone is making a fuss of something.

The commotion will relate to something stupid. The play, perhaps.

He is able to listen as he walks downstairs.

From down below, you can hear Rosalind's voice.

Her voice is loud enough to be heard from the second floor landing.

In fact, there are two voices.

When he finds Rosalind, she is standing in the hall.

You can see what the shouting is all about.

Keith is there.

The Keith in front of him is different than before. What happened to the knitted beanie hat?

Keith is wearing a denim jacket, which makes him look older, less cool, and more obviously depressed. There is something sad about it all. That's until he remembers what Keith has done.

He points towards Keith and says, 'Out.'

'Oh, great,' Keith says. 'What's your moral position, Joe?'

'Get out.'

'We all want to know.'

'Out.'

'You haven't told me your moral position.'

'Come on,' Rosalind says and opens the front door.

In a moment like this, he would usually step aside. This is different. If he were to step closer, he might throw a punch. Hostility towards men is a condition of being a father.

Why did Keith come? It must have been to make amends.

It would be nice if he could wish this man away, and imagine Keith never came. It would be nice, but it wouldn't be true.

It's a sudden, welcome surprise to see the door close shut.

He has achieved something, at least. Something unexpected.

He is able to step forward and let Rosalind relax into his arms.

As a father, there are certain things you should do. It's important to hug.

What he hadn't noticed is that George is standing a couple of feet away. In the living room, George is leaning against the wall.

'Come here,' George says, putting an arm on Rosalind's shoulder.

It's a short while until they let each other go.

You get the impression they must have talked about Keith. What did George do?

'George was very calm,' Rosalind says.

George is smiling, like a child who deserves a reward.

'I just asked what his problem was,' George says. 'I should probably have kept quiet.'

'No,' Rosalind says. 'You were calm.'

George was calm. Rosalind wasn't.

She is trying to make a smile of it. She is not doing well. However much she wants to smile, she can't manage it. You can tell by the look on her face. Her skin is paler than before. You can see, right there, some of the pain Keith has caused. It's her dignity that makes the situation worse. She shouldn't have to rely on dignity. It should be natural for her to cry.

What did Keith want? When you put the question to Rosalind, her expression reverts to neutral mode.

'He wanted to explain himself.'

'Did you mention the guesthouse?'

She is nodding whilst looking at the floor.

'He wants to come home.'

'And will you let him?'

'No.'

She mumbles something else. She mentions how she might go to bed.

Now that Keith has made an appearance, and been dismissed, there is nothing else that could threaten the project. It has all been decided. Rosalind, out of some kind of moral certainty, has turned Keith away. She has made the decision;

she is sticking with it. Don't expect her to change her mind.

*

He has no motivation to pull the covers from his body the next morning.

This is the dazed period after sleeping in which you can't shake off a dream - whatever it was. You can't make sense of anything.

There is nothing but silence.

What will Rosalind and George be doing?

From what he can tell, the play is coming along well. If the house is silent, the actors are thinking. If there is laughter, the actors are rehearsing. This is the life of the house.

He passes down the staircase, and, whistling a nonsense tune, walks towards the studio.

In the studio, of all places, there is life at last. It's no longer an abandoned room. You can tell as much from the cigarettes in the ashtray. Rosalind has been smoking, which is good. She likes to smoke when she paints.

A half painted canvas is resting on the easel. What happened to the thin line of blue? It looks fuller now. The swan has acquired a shade of grey since he last saw it. You can see the pencilled outline of seagulls, some rocks, and a harbour waiting to be drawn. She has been working on it. She is a creator of things. She knows how to make things beautiful. In this respect, she is a genius.

It makes him glad that she didn't burn more. Only some of it was burnt. The hardest, most painful stuff was given to the fire. Without him, she might have burnt it all. This has been his only contribution to the world of art. Without running himself down, it would be fair to say he knows nothing about the subject.

There is a photograph of a man kneeling on the floor with a kind of exploding heart.

There is a whistle on a piece of string, which must have

come from the march.

What else is there?

The cobwebs are gone. You could even think of the room as a workplace, and not just somewhere she likes to keep things. It's somewhere you could imagine Rosalind working with a cigarette, and something to read.

There is a sense that if he stays in the studio too long, he might disturb something.

The sign is what he came for. His duty is to gather the sign, which Rosalind has finished. It's a square Bevan Breakfast sign with a thick piece of wood. It's similar to what you would see when a house is for sale.

Ordinarily, the task of erecting a sign would be outsourced to someone with skill. He felt it was time he should rise to the challenge. It's rare that he assumes responsibility for things.

There is work to do.

There is no-one in the hall and no-one in the kitchen. He must do the job himself.

From the toolbox he pulls out a hammer.

It seems obvious where the sign must go. Long before you arrive at the gate, you should be able to see it from the pavement. Everyone should know about Bevan Breakfast. If nothing else, people will say that the sign looks good. This matters to some people.

*

On the front lawn he positions the sign against the fence.

He pinches the nail with his thumb and forefinger.

The nail is placed into position.

With his left hand he balances the slat, and with his right, aims the hammer.

He taps the hammer against the nail.

The nail sinks deep into the wood.

There.

It's only afterwards, looking at the house, that he allows

himself to smile.

Look at the house.

Rosalind is staring from the bedroom window. She acknowledges him with a wave; she draws the curtains.

*

The red bottle of wine, which he was saving for a celebration, is ready to be opened. They can drink it between the four of them.

He brings four wine glasses and places them on the kitchen table.

It became obvious that he should call a meeting. He thought it was something they should do. It seemed like a good idea.

It will be a celebration more than a meeting. The house is ready. If there was a list, there would be nothing left to tick off. Everything is done. Bevan Breakfast has started to resemble a place worth visiting.

It has been a success just to get everyone sitting around the kitchen table.

Rosalind is wearing a black and white striped top. If you stuck a beret on her head she would make a perfect stereotype. An easel, too, would complete the picture.

Rosalind is the person he is most grateful for. There are moments you choose to remember about people. With Rosalind, he remembers the moment she let him inside. She didn't have to open the door. It was for no reason other than kindness – or perhaps pity – that she did so.

George is wearing red trouser braces, which might seem decidedly un-George, until you remember that George's dress sense has no relationship to his personality. George is less complicated than his clothes would suggest.

Daryl is even simpler, without wanting to be belittling. You get the sense that Daryl will be happy so long as he can watch football in the living room.

The canvas in the hall will justify his own presence. He has

PR appeal, as George senior said. Let them look at his face.

When it comes to the matter of talking, he realises there are plenty of things to say.

'I just want to say thank you, everyone.'

This is just the beginning.

He mentions that he doesn't know how long he will live here. In the event that Rosalind should ask him to stay indefinitely, he will happily do so. Muriel might even join them one day.

'I think we can build something together. I want to use this house as a resource for those less fortunate. We can rebuild lives.'

When you spell it out in words, it all sounds easy. A concept is easier than its execution. It would be better if he could live his life as a concept.

'We're going to show the world how to live passionately, and sincerely, and with a collective spirit.'

It's true, what he said. It makes him want to carry on talking with passion.

'We'll welcome the guests like they're our brothers and sisters.'

Of course, it's impossible to know what the guests will be like until they arrive. Until then, we will assume they're angels.

'And let me say thanks to Daryl for being our guinea pig.'

Daryl is smiling at the mention of this. In truth, the involvement of Daryl will extend to performing whichever tasks are assigned to him. That's the role of the vole.

The guesthouse will work itself out. You can't guess what will happen. The best attitude is to enjoy it all.

Rosalind has been waiting to speak. It was impolite to ignore her for so long. She smiles, letting everyone know she has been waiting to interrupt.

'We're having a party,' she says.

'Oh, right.'

'We've invited loads of people.'

The party, which Rosalind hadn't mentioned until now, is scheduled for the night of the launch. There is so much to organise and he will be responsible for none of it.

What will his role be?

There is a part of him that wants to ask, 'what should I do?'

No, don't. It would sound too pathetic.

Besides, his face is the important thing.

Rosalind opens a diary and says, 'What drink do you want?'

'Anything.'

'I'll make some cocktails,' George says.

'What do you drink?' Rosalind says in the direction of Daryl.

Daryl says that he likes beer.

George says that he will prepare the food.

They decide upon beetroot salad and vol-au-vents. Daryl will make some sandwiches.

Rosalind says she has sorted the entertainment.

For Rosalind and George, the priority is the live music. Between the two of them there is enough youth and creative passion to make it a success.

Rosalind looks at her father and says, 'You can throw some shapes.'

There is laughter.

There is a worry in his mind. The worry is just a small thing.

'Is Muriel coming?'

'I don't think so,' Rosalind says. 'Why don't you ask her?'

'I thought you might have done.'

If there was a drawing board, he would be consulting it, without a clue as to what to do next. And when he is certain there is nothing else to say, he chooses instead to pour another glass.

Thirteen

When it's established where the furniture will be moved and how long the food will take to prepare, he can begin to envisage the party itself. He has an idea of what it will be like, but it's just an idea. It might be fun, if he allows himself to relax. He will probably be the oldest person there. It's important to prepare for this.

The main hope is to avoid disaster. In fact, the party will be a success if it's anything less than disastrous. That's about as much as you can hope for. Failure is fine, in the short term. He can cope with it, even if this time he has a reason to believe otherwise.

It's exciting, and scary, to think about what might happen. How many people will show up? It's impossible to know. It will raise some money, which is the important thing.

The party will be more than just a celebration. If a party can have a cause, it would resemble something like this.

There is music. It comes from the living room, where Rosalind is pressing buttons on the hi-fi. As you walk in, if you turn to the left there's a space in the corner where the guests, no doubt, will dance.

George looks at the floor and says to Rosalind that yes, there is enough room for a drum kit.

From the hall comes the sound of the doorbell.

There is no debate as to who should answer the door.

Rosalind walks.

The front door opens; he can hear the feigned enthusiasm

of a stressed host.

'Hello! Come in.'

What is he feeling? It's something close to nervousness, even though his immediate job is to carry out a simple task. He must say hello.

'Just in here,' Rosalind says, leading the musicians into the living room.

From what he can tell, they are older than Rosalind, but younger than him.

The guests enter the living room and put down their instruments.

It doesn't occur to them to take off their shoes.

Is he going to stand here for much longer?

The guy with the leather jacket reaches out and says, 'Sorry mate, what's your name?'

'Joe.'

'I'm Dom,' the lad says. 'How do you know Rosalind?'

'I'm her father.'

Dom looks ahead and says, 'Good stuff.'

There is nothing wrong with Dom, as such. The lad is harmless, and bright enough to make a conversation with a stranger. You could say that Dom is being friendly. However, the friendliness probably owes more to a hatred of silence on Dom's part.

Dom says that Rosalind often comes to their shows.

Then Dom mentions some mutual friends of theirs, none of whom sound familiar.

What about the other musicians? One is sitting on the armrest.

Another guy is speaking on his mobile phone, instructing someone on how they can find the house.

He is aware of the need to raise his game. What is he offering? Not much. In this crowd, he offers nothing.

'Thanks for coming,' he says, smiling for them.

'It's a cool house,' Dom says, distracted by the band mates, who are laughing at something.

There is no point in talking anymore.

As he walks into the hall, he listens to the voices behind him.

'Let's order a pizza.'

'I'm starving, man.'

And of course, you can't walk through the hall without seeing his face. There it is. His face on the wall. It feels wrong that the face isn't frowning.

The expectation is that he will entertain. This is what they came for.

He can see the shape of two small women through the front door glass. Their faces are alive with something.

'Hello!'

Americans.

'Wow,' says the one who smiles the most. 'This is incredible.'

'Come inside.'

Despite their smiles, they won't understand the significance of their visit. They are the first paying guests. Do they know how long it took to make this plan? Not very long, but it has been a difficult road.

The feeling of welcoming the guests was just as he imagined. It was exciting, and scary. This cannot be helped.

They give him their coats, which he places on the banister.

He leads them into the living room, where the strangers are laughing at the television.

Someone is shouting for pizza.

The music stops. It starts again. The doorbell rings. Someone answers. The feigned enthusiasm…

*

What is he supposed to do?

All he can think of doing is to hover in the kitchen. That's the only thing.

What else?

There is plenty of cooking to be done.

Already, some of the food has been laid on the table. There is a lasagne from the high street deli.

There is nothing wrong with the idea of chopping onions. In fact, he came into the kitchen with the intention of helping out.

'It's alright,' Rosalind says. 'We've done most of it.'

'What can I do then?'

'Nothing.'

He ought to do something, really.

What about the burgers?

He lifts the tray and scrapes the burgers onto a plate.

From the fridge he pulls out a bag of lettuce. The lettuce is no good.

He rips open the pack of sausages and snips them apart.

He is able to stare through the kitchen window, above the lawn and the wood…

Look out from the window and you can see Daryl working on the hammock. It's where you would expect it to be, just at the bottom of the garden where the grass disappears and becomes dry mud. The hammock is there, suspended between two trees, with half the sling yet to be woven.

You can see people on the lawn. He can see that most of them are young: twenty-six, twenty-seven, twenty-eight… although the musicians are about forty.

At some point, he will be more sociable. It's about making a plan for survival.

*

There is music coming from the patio, where there was no music before. What's the song? He's not familiar with it. He doesn't even know how you would describe it.

Without much thought, he carries the plate of burgers across the lawn.

Everyone is talking about something different.

You can hear someone talking about London.

At the bottom of the garden, he can see that Daryl is focused on the hammock.

There are plenty of nice things he could say about Daryl.

Daryl is a polite boy. A shy, kind boy who isn't loved enough by the world. You wonder where his mother might be, but that's a subject for another day.

He has a quick conversation with Daryl about burgers.

He is made to linger, conscious that he has nothing substantial to say.

And Daryl says, 'Have you met Rosalind's friends before?'

'Not these ones.'

He looks at the guests on the lawn.

The guests are laughing at something. He doesn't know what they're laughing at.

Daryl is examining the hammock. 'Do you miss your wife?'

It requires a moment's thought. 'Of course. But such is life, Daryl. I don't really allow myself to think about it.'

'Why not?'

'I'd prefer to let it fester.'

'Fester?'

'Like something rotting.'

Look at the plate. He can see that the burgers might get cold. Nobody wants his food.

There is someone behind him. It's a man with thick-rimmed glasses who says, 'Have you got any veggie ones?'

'I can check.'

'No, it's all right,' the man says. 'I'm supposed to be meeting a girl in a second.'

The man pulls out his mobile phone. 'I did a shoot with her last night. What do you think?'

On the screen is a woman in a red dress.

You can't deny she is pretty. There must have been some effort behind the prettiness.

'That's nice.'

'I'm going to ask her out.'

'Do it.'

One of the Americans reaches out for a burger.

There is a boyfriend, too.

The lad is wearing glasses, but not thick-rimmed ones.

It's true that the girlfriend looks like a cheerleader and her boyfriend a scientist. No doubt the boyfriend is tender and loyal - and perhaps even, a brilliant scientist. But that's what they look like.

'I love this house,' she says. 'It's totally how I imagined. Look at this cute little garden.'

There is nothing to say, except to acknowledge that the house is nice.

Then she says, 'My dad would never do something this cool.'

*

The kitchen is where he wants to be. Despite the amount of people in the kitchen, you can pretend to be doing something. The kettle. The microwave. These are things to cherish.

He decides to stand next to the telephone. It gives the impression that he has something to do. He would rather stand and look at the telephone.

It would be hard to walk anywhere, if he wanted to. There are too many people. It would require a conversation along the way. It's hard to get involved in any conversation because he doesn't have the chance to participate. Their preferred method of interaction is to broadcast. A couple of times someone's said 'thank you', and walked ahead. Thank you for letting us bring the party. We won't make a mess. No-one has envisaged that he could make his own mess if he wanted. The expectation is that he will be the worried parent, whose involvement should be to barricade himself upstairs and only come down once it's all over.

A man wearing a trilby steps forward, introducing himself

by the initial E. This E describes himself as a singer in a band. The guy says he lives in Camberwell, and that it's good he lives in Camberwell because it means he's not living in Nunhead. The singer's state of mind – altered by something – means that he presents all this information in a rambling burst. The lad talks about how it's great to live in zone 2, and how zone 2 is a lot better than zone 3. Don't even mention zones 4, 5 and 6. It transpires, after a few questions back and forth, that the lad was raised in East Sussex, which causes him to bow his head, like it's something to be ashamed about. The lad doesn't want to discuss it any further. London is his goldfish bowl.

The conversation doesn't happen. The singer is waiting for him to say something.

What should he say?

There are questions he would like to ask. Like, how do you know you're any good?

He doesn't say this.

'I've just got back from Berlin,' the singer says.

'What were you doing there?'

'I was performing.'

The singer says that everyone seems to love him in Germany.

It doesn't seem fair that he should have to listen to the singer.

The telephone gives him something to look at.

He lifts the receiver, just so he can do something.

Should he pretend to make a call? The guilt will not last long.

Then he notices that E has gone.

How much does he dislike these people? He wouldn't like to think they're normal. No, there is nothing normal about them.

If it was his own party, things would be different. There is something to be said for setting some ground rules. No morons allowed. That's it, really. Everything else is permissable.

A woman is standing against the fridge. She has short, boyish hair - what you might call a Joan of Arc look. What does this say about her? Nothing.

She is wearing boots that are loose around the ankle.

She remains next to the fridge, which causes her to apologise after he opens it for nothing.

She looks around and says, 'What you're doing is so inspiring.'

'Thank you.'

She smiles. 'That's all I wanted to say.'

The challenge is to keep her in front of him. Hopefully she likes burgers.

Just say something.

'We've got a long way to go.'

'But you've made a great start,' she says. 'You should be proud.'

She looks at him like he's a hero. If nothing else, he should be proud of this.

It's doubtful that he is deserving of the praise. It's absurd, in fact.

His main focus is on the words.

He doesn't want to decide how lovely she is. He hasn't corroborated the evidence, but the evidence is there. A small button nose. She has freckles on her cheeks; a dot-to-dot puzzle, not that he wants to draw a line on her face.

There is a danger that she'll go and stand somewhere else. She will praise someone else.

There is someone behind. It's the man in thick-rimmed glasses.

The man has a cigarette in his mouth and says, 'Shit man, where's my lighter gone?'

The man puts a hand on the woman's back. 'Let's go, Annabel,' says the man, who is doing a bad job of hiding his impatience.

The moron has got what he wanted.

What's the most practical way of concealing his sadness?

He has enough about him to shake the photographer's hand.

Annabel – as she is now called – pulls on her jacket and says, 'Do you smoke?'

'No, I'm alright.'

'You're sensible. Well, it was lovely meeting you.'

'And you.'

It's not clear why she's leaving. It's impossible to guess.

Then, from the garden door, she turns around and looks at him.

Is that a smile?

It might be his imagination. She might have just smelt something and scrunched her face. She might have remembered something she wanted to forget. It's too much to think about.

At some stage, everyone will pity him. He is hopeful that he can inspire pity.

He opens the fridge. The beer makes him feel ill.

Everything is getting louder.

He can hear a debate among the band members. They want everyone to move into the living room.

One of them cheers.

Another laughs.

In the short while he has been in the kitchen, they have used words like 'retard' and 'gypsy'. He can't imagine why anyone would talk like this. He would prefer them not to speak, unless, as someone once said, what they speak of is more beautiful than silence itself.

What should he do?

As much as he would like to stand in front of the telephone, he ought to make an appearance in the living room. In fact, he ought to say a few words. He should say hello, and welcome. That way, everyone can put a face to a name. *The* face, in fact. It would be good to introduce them to the face.

Until now, he hadn't thought that he might make a speech. What will he say? It won't be an organised speech. It will be something spontaneous. He should thank everyone for their presence, assuming they care about the cause. He will make a joke about his personal circumstances. It will allow them to relax in his presence.

*

A crowd of about thirty has squeezed into the living room. If you were to judge them by their clothes, you could hardly tell them apart. There are lots of slogan t-shirts.

Someone is wearing goggles like a strange, aquatic creature.

If these people are about anything, they are about irony.

No one has spoken to him. This might be for numerical reasons. Perhaps everyone is occupied. It might be for deeper reasons.

In the middle is Rosalind. She is laughing at something.

George is closer to the front, speaking to the Americans, who, like Rosalind, are laughing at something.

The musicians are positioned close to the window.

The guitarist is looking down, thumbing the strings.

The drummer is wearing jeans but no t-shirt at all. This means you can see the coloured tattoos all the way up his arms and neck. You can't imagine the drummer being anything other than drunk, or fucked on drugs.

The singer, Dom, is wearing a black chequered shirt with one half tucked inside his jeans. This is what genius looks like.

It would be better to speak now. It would be better to say something before they're all drunk. He had better speak for Rosalind. He had better speak for the house and make everything alright.

In the old days, he was good at making speeches. It seems more problematic now. He should imagine that he's addressing someone like Annabel, someone he would like to talk to. He should make his presence known.

Why doesn't he tell a joke? It won't be funny. It will just be the sort of thing he should probably say.

'Don't worry guys,' he says, moving to the front. 'I'm not going to sing.'

It doesn't get a laugh.

'Alright, everyone. Thanks for coming today.'

When he said, 'alright, everyone', the words sounded calmer than he expected.

'We have a donation hat on the side. Please be generous.'

There is a whoop from the back.

He is able to pitch a steady voice.

'You've all played a big part in the launch of Bevan,' he says. 'I don't pretend that our ambition is not a huge one. Our aim is to help homeless people, and those experiencing financial difficulty. We want to listen to them; we want to give them a chance. Every time I see a young man or woman sleeping in a doorway, or in a park… or in a hospital waiting room… it reminds me of why we're here. Don't give up on them.'

There is another whoop from the middle. It's like a rally, with supporters he doesn't like very much.

'I mean this sincerely, ladies and gentlemen. You've helped us make a positive start. But there is so much more to do.'

He continues to say that he hopes everyone will enjoy the music. That's all.

The room is silent.

He doesn't give them anything. It's not essential that he should smile.

Where is the applause?

If anything, everyone looks embarrassed on his behalf.

Admittedly, Rosalind is smiling. George is clapping on his own.

One or two others begin to clap.

Then it stops.

When you look at the audience you think, where's the anger? No one cares. No one wants to listen.

The music starts with a drum roll. Then comes the bass. Then it all happens. It frees everyone to the point where they can dance.

The first song passes over him. It has the effect of making him feel distant, hermetically sealed from the crowd.

What is he doing? He is standing alone.

He listens to another song and finds nothing of interest. He can manage one more.

His eyes are drawn more to the crowd than the musicians.

There is dancing, but little sweat. All of them seem conscious of what they're doing. You couldn't dance in a more idle way.

Rosalind is doing nothing.

George is standing just opposite Rosalind, leaning onto her shoulder. There is a hand on her waist. It belongs to George.

Rosalind is smiling. She allows the hand to remain on her waist.

Oh dear.

There is a moment in which nothing seems to happen. George is whispering something. That's as much as you can see.

It's not like he can stand and watch. It's not like he can object, either. It has nothing to do with him.

All that's certain is that he should probably leave the room.

Don't think about it, Joe.

Just enjoy the party.

*

You forget how awful they are until you enter the kitchen again. He approaches some of the guests, but upon hearing a glimpse of conversation – something about London – decides his time would be better spent elsewhere.

What are they saying about London? Nothing, really. Their wish is that London reflects well on them. Everything that's good about the city must, in some indirect way, reflect on them too. They want to embody London. They want to be London.

His main thought is to look around and think, who's next? Someone will approach him and say something awful. He wants to point a finger and say 'I don't like you, I don't like you, and I definitely don't like you.' He could spend a good part of the night doing precisely this. It wouldn't reflect well on him, though.

There is no reason to remain downstairs. He could start a conversation, but why bother? There is no contingency plan.

On the other side is Daryl.

Daryl is scraping some rice into the bin.

There is a stack of dirty plates, which Daryl has brought upon himself to clean.

It would be nice to help out. First, it would be nice to let Daryl know he's not alone.

And second, it will allow him to avoid everyone else.

'Do you want a hand?'

'No, I'm alright,' says Daryl, who appears to believe the only emotion you should express in such a situation is complete surprise.

'Are you sure?'

'Positive.'

That's about as far as he can take it.

In fact, it feels like he's troubling Daryl just by standing there.

All Daryl would like is to put his head down and scrub some plates.

*

The way upstairs is more treacherous than he could have anticipated. There are women he doesn't recognise; one of them is looking at him like she ought to know him from somewhere.

Where should he go next?

There is the bathroom. It's somewhere he could stand for a moment, just to give up some time. It's better than downstairs.

No, he should continue to walk, even if the stairs present their own dangers. He should do what it takes, so long as he can find a pillow and a mattress. Sleep is what inspires him.

He climbs the staircase with an idea in his mind. The idea is that he should keep climbing stairs, until he reaches the sky or something.

On the landing is a woman whose hair is like nothing he's ever seen. It's wrapped and pinned in what looks like a bandana. It's like a dead skunk. A dead skunk on her head.

A couple of people are sitting on the steps, focusing on each other. All the while, the music is loud. The floor is almost shaking.

If he could choose the best kind of evening, it wouldn't be like this. It would be quite different. He would stay in bed, if it were possible. A bed is an emotionless place.

*

The door opens and he enters the bedroom. It's the same bedroom as all the other days.

If it were possible, he would barricade the door and wrap the room with razor wire. But then it becomes harder to envisage why he would do such a thing. Why indeed, when all he wanted from this project was to stare society in the face, not shoo it away. What kind of house does he want to build? Should it not be a house for all people, even morons?

There is plenty to think about. He would like it to be morning; he would like to see daylight.

He is almost glad about the music below. Silence would give him too much time to think. There is plenty of noise. The music, and the accompanying beat, is the soundtrack to everything.

In the bedroom, nobody can see him. Nobody can see that he is beginning to undress.

He unbuckles the belt of his jeans.

On the floor is a pile of underpants, which is where he throws down the jeans.

The socks come next.

Then he positions himself under the duvet.

It has been a while since he washed the bed linen.

It almost makes him want to get up, but the thought of carrying his dirty linen into the kitchen is too much.

He flicks off the lamp.

Go away, lamplight. Darkness should surround him.

Like always, he is tired. Tonight he is more tired than usual.

It seems pointless to sigh, because sighing would be the done thing. Better to laugh. Laughter can help.

And then he sighs.

What brought him to the house? It was so he could build something.

The premise, of course, is that everything will eventually come good. The project is still there. He must stick to it. He must throw himself into the life of the house.

The reason for coming upstairs was to get away from everything. Sleep is the get-out-of-jail card. It can remove him from the house and the party. The night has come at last.

What else should he think about?

The war! He had forgotten about the war. If you spend five minutes with the guests, you could almost forget there was anything bad in the world.

What war?

You can bet none of these people attended the march.

Meanwhile, what was he doing?

That's right - he was sitting at home in front of the television. The march was happening on his screen. It was something that happened within recent memory.

There was a fuss about whether he should go. Without saying it in so many words, Rosalind thought he should come along. George was more relaxed on the subject. Between the two of them, they made him feel like a bastard. And perhaps they were right! There was a reason for his absence, wasn't there? The trouble was that he was scared of seeing Muriel. That was a situation he was keen to avoid.

The terrible thing is that he has plenty of time to think about Muriel. He didn't ask for this time. He doesn't want it. But here it is - time, and darkness, in which to think about Muriel. Are these thoughts born of love? Fear, more like. It would be better to feel love.

He can cope with loneliness, but this is different.

He wonders, as well, whether Muriel has these thoughts. Does she too, lie awake at night and think of him? He would like to know the answer. He wouldn't be able to tell you.

Is there anything else to worry about?

What about Rosalind?

Rosalind and George.

Imagine what George and Rosalind must be doing right now!

Relax, Joe. Don't be boring. Let them do whatever they want to do.

No, there is nothing to worry about.

She is drunk, but intelligent, and so is George. There is no harm to be done.

So why does it bother him?

Part Three

Fourteen

For Barry Jack Thorne, his home, an ex-local authority apartment in the outskirts of town, does not match his own view of himself. When he describes it to others as the outskirts, they must imagine that it's somewhere green and quiet. This would be wrong.

The road is flanked by two estates, both of which are compact, brick in composition, and, if you wanted to push it, art deco. It's a modest place to live, without being ugly, and without being beautiful.

About a hundred yards away is the motorway, which is ugly, but highly useful. The noise from the motorway is, to his knowledge, perpetual. It doesn't ever quieten down, not even at night. It's like living under a flight path with the jet engines brought to street level. Sometimes he wonders where all these cars are going. They don't seem to have a destination.

In a bigger, more exciting town or city, you could be forgiven for thinking the location was ideal. Unfortunately, the town is not exciting. The town was never beautiful. It was a shipbuilding town, which is no longer the case. The economy is dead. There is talk of a shopping centre opening, which would retrieve things somewhat.

What brought him here? It was the promise of cheap property, and the sense it made to buy a cheap home. It made sense to buy somewhere cheap and pay down the debt. It made sense at the time.

One thing you can say about the town is that things seem

to work. If you leave your rubbish at the gate, someone will collect it. If you ring the police, they will get to you eventually. There is a general sense of order, which is something to be welcomed amid the chaos of living. The town doesn't attract many visitors, but the residents, to their credit, want to stop it from falling apart.

There is a path that runs underneath the building, as if the building were positioned on stilts. The path is kept tidy, but you wouldn't want to walk here at night. Some of the lamps are broken, which makes everything darker than it ought to be.

There is a bronze plaque, which he has never taken the time to read.

The entrance is a hollow metal door with a yellow-painted trim.

There are eight buttons on the intercom, none of which bear a name.

When you step inside, it has a momentary chilling effect, when you realise you might as well be outside. If you were to judge the building upon entering the stairwell, you would consider it a dank little place.

He has seen the stairwell enough times to seal the image in his mind. The yellow painted brick is cheerful enough. The floor is concrete, which gives you the sense of walking in a multi-storey car park.

There is a message from the Green Party taped to the brick, which, like the yellow paint, is all well and good.

It's only when you open the door to the apartment that you realise it's just like any other home. In front of him is the narrow corridor, along which there is a toilet, office and bedroom, where his wife is asleep. The rooms are spacious enough because the building dates from 1948, when spaciousness was allowed.

The kitchen is separated from everything else. You can imagine that five or six people could fit inside (although this has never been put to the test). There is a litter tray on the floor, and a stand on which the cat can dig its claws.

The apartment doesn't get much natural light, except in the lounge where the large, single-pane window keeps him hot in the summer and freezing in the winter.

The lounge has been afforded as much love as you could give a room.

In the corner is a grandfather clock that once belonged to his father.

A cabinet contains models of old ships.

There is a cushioned basket, where the cat is lying on its paws.

All these items are important, but perhaps this building doesn't deserve to contain them.

He stares through the window, beyond the square lawns of the estate.

A heap of rubbish has been allowed to mount and fester in the basement garden. It's a pile of broken furniture, paint pots and bin bags. The smell has been rising.

Despite all this, the estate is a solid community. It's a combination of honest, decent folk who post each other's mail under the door – because the lock to the post room is broken – and young villains who smoke in the stairwells, let off fire extinguishers and sometimes, boot their footballs against the doors. There are residents meetings in which the adults discuss these problems and whether the landlords will do anything. The consensus, most of the time, comes with a sigh.

Barry tosses the magazine onto the coffee table.

On the table is a bottle of wine, which was bought for reasons of guilt. You might call it a peace offering. It's just a little something to say sorry, and to say congratulations, Mr Street. Congratulations, because you got some praise in a magazine, which didn't seem possible a month and a half ago. And sorry, for the way in which we parted, which was a shame.

The magazine – which had only been brought to his attention yesterday – has a feature on Bevan Breakfast. If you look further down, there is a picture of a canvas. You can see

Joe depicted as a work of art. In one paragraph, the project is described as a social enterprise, then a commune, then a vanity project, and finally, a beacon of hope. It mentions the paintings, which are supposed to be excellent. It claims there is something San Francisco about it all. The tone of the article, on the whole, is a kind of sycophantic awe. It says:

Look beyond the pretty pictures, and the real story is of a man reborn. Bevan Breakfast... represents the reincarnation of Street as a political and moral force for good.

In hindsight, he would rather not have punched Joe on the nose. At the time, it felt like the right thing to do. He hadn't realised the implications of it.

The truth is that he has never had a client like Joe. The resistance was something remarkable. With most clients, they succumb to his demands without thinking. They want money and prestige and to be famous for the right reasons. It was different with Joe.

The whole episode had caused Barry, with some alarm, to reassess his approach to things. Perhaps integrity does exist. Remember what Thorne & Glover Associates once stood for. It had been a successful public relations agency, until it went the way of everything else. Then it became Thorne Associates, without the Glover.

So what next?

It should be his priority to make amends. It would be the decent thing.

Most of all, he should be humble enough to congratulate Joe on what has been an incredible success.

Somehow, Joe has made something for himself. Joe, who gave the impression as someone to whom the world had done great harm, has finally won. The world had battered Joe to the point where, at fifty-nine, he was timid, gentle in his ways, and exhausted. It had forced him to change, and change again, to the point where he had no alternative but to win at last. The man must be happy, or working towards happiness. In this solitary pursuit, Joe has achieved what no-one expected. No-one could have predicted it. You would have got long odds, were it possible to bet on such a thing.

Fifteen

It's still a good time to be Joe Street. It has still been a vindication of his character. He is a credible, legitimate person who can be listened to again. He must be owed a hundred apologies, but never mind. Freedom is enough.

He walks to the window and realises that he hasn't even opened the curtains.

The bedroom is a place that has become too familiar.

It's a strange feeling to have nothing to do, and to be here, making the bed again, where he thought he would spend so little time.

The room is clean, to an extent. He wanted to keep a certain order to things.

For five or six nights, everything has been difficult. The parties have been loud. On each occasion, the music has pumped out from the living room. The floorboards have throbbed with it. Strangers have made a habit of knocking on his bedroom door. It has been an exercise in survival.

The partygoers, from what he can tell, have included the hardcore of regulars. Each night has seen an increase in visitors, which you would think is a good thing. Unfortunately, the numbers are swelling to the point where things are getting intolerable. They will have to reduce the numbers, which is a shame. The ethos, after all, was to include everyone.

There is nothing rotten or immoral about what has happened.

There has been no fighting, no theft, no damage to the

walls or trouble at the door. There is nothing wrong with any of it. It just compels him, for whatever reason, to keep the door shut.

*

It's only now, as he places his foot on the creaking step, that he notices the silence of the house. Living here, you almost forget that silence does exist. To walk through the house, in the silence, is something extraordinary.

He opens the living room door. What motivates him is curiosity.

Someone is lying on the couch, which is unfortunate.

Someone is slumped against the wall.

There is someone kneeling with a bucket of hot water, and who, to her credit, apologises for the carpet stain.

This is the worst of it. A polite kind of wreckage.

*

At least everyone in the kitchen is awake.

The newest guests are two women from… where was it? Germany, or Austria, maybe. The eldest is sitting at the table, leaning on a sheet of paper. The youngest, with a bow in her hair, is laughing with someone.

George and Rosalind are sitting together. There is no immediate difference in their act. It's not as though his presence has changed anything.

Under the table, you can see their hands are apart. Actually, they're not even close to touching.

There is a copy of the script on the table.

When you think about it, there is plenty to keep George and Rosalind busy. The play. The guesthouse. Their love.

But is it love?

In truth, he hasn't spent long enough downstairs to know whether Rosalind and George are in love. From what he has seen, the love only seems to exist when they're drunk. The art, though, requires them to be sober. Rosalind paints, and George writes, but only in daylight hours. The alcohol is what consumes them at night.

On the table is a pack of flyers. The words *Bevan Breakfast* are embossed in large letters. Look closer and it says, *Art. Literature. Music. Film.* It has a Peter Brook quotation about theatre being an empty space. It's the sort of thing someone would give away on a street corner. Well done to Rosalind, whose eye for colour is undeniable.

There is a magazine folded open.

In fact, it's one of those street newspapers sold by the homeless.

In the caption it describes the members of Bevan Breakfast as belonging to a set. It has a picture of the canvas in the hall. Just below, you can make out the words:

… the real story is of a man reborn.

And then he stops reading.

How did this happen?

'We gave them some pictures,' Rosalind says.

Then George says, 'Would you like us to make a comment?'

'No.'

'Everyone's talking about you,' Rosalind says. 'They mentioned you on the radio.'

'On the radio?'

'Yes, as a kind of footnote. But still.'

He always knew how the media would spin it. Look who's making a recovery!

He will regard the media not just at arm's length, but rather through the lens of a telescope.

George says, 'How do you want to play it?'

'There's nothing to play.'

'You don't want to give an interview?'

'No.'

George, whose self-conscious cardigan befits a man in love, has nothing else to say.

'That's alright,' Rosalind says. 'I understand.'

She is looking at him, which makes him think that maybe she does understand.

'It's just that we've already arranged something,' she says.

'What?'

'An interview.'

A headache is coming on. He can feel his right foot doing something, perhaps not twitching but definitely wriggling in a way that suggests it's time to leave.

Then he notices something that, in truth, he doesn't have the words for. The surprise is not so much what he can see, but the fact that he hadn't noticed. Just behind the door is a woman sitting on a stool. She is looking at no-one. It's almost like she's sitting for her own benefit, with no regard for the work of art she will become. She is naked.

With his eyes, he chooses to pass over the details of her body.

The guests, and the strangers at the table, continue to draw what they see.

It doesn't feel like he should be sitting here. It's not something he should have permission for. After all, he has no artistic talent. The others understand what they're looking at. It's the body of a woman, sure, but what does it mean beyond that? He doesn't know, which is why he shouldn't be sitting here. It's impossible to interpret what's in front of him. He looks at the woman as he would look upon any living thing. Everyone else can see something different.

You wouldn't notice just by entering the room that a life drawing class is taking place. You would have to wait a minute or so, like he did, before you noticed anything. You wouldn't notice just by looking at George, who is still talking to Rosalind. You would have to turn around and look at the body.

For a moment, George and Rosalind seem happier talking

to each other than the alternative, which is to look at the body on the stool.

It seems more obvious now why the house was silent.

It's like he has entered a meeting and been instructed – without it being said in so many words – to sit in silence. Just sit down and do nothing. That would be the best thing.

*

For the next however many hours, his contact with the house is minimal. His instinct was to come upstairs and shut himself away. The plan was to stand on the balcony, and bask in his own magnificence. It has worked.

From his position on the balcony, he is able to watch what he needs.

What can he see?

The rehearsals are happening on the lawn.

There is something peaceful about watching it all. It gives him a chance to listen and not be noticed.

From listening to the voices, he can recognise the actors.

One of the men is almost shouting.

The young woman, whose hair is like straw, has more power in her voice than you would think.

From the balcony, of course, there is only so much you can understand. Every third or forth line is difficult to hear. It's hard to distinguish between the lines and the real conversations. Even so, it's nice just to look at the actors and watch their movements.

The cast have found a rhythm. The lines are landing as they ought to. The words are being pronounced as words should be when attached to meaning, not as alien, unfamiliar things. To whom this improvement can be credited is unclear. It probably came from Rosalind.

George, in his cardigan, is watching the actors from the patio side of the lawn.

Rosalind is standing amid the actors. She is just the

director, though.

George is saying something. He is telling a joke, as if to mildly embarrass Rosalind but ultimately say no, come on, you're wonderful.

There is laughter. It makes him feel more alone.

Then he wonders whether he should do something to help. Despite his lack of creativity, and skill, there might be a role for him. What could he do? In theory, he could carry the props. He could fetch what they need.

But actually, this is a bad idea. More than anything the actors would make him conscious of his own irrelevance. In a practical sense, he offers nothing. His contribution would extend to making comments about how nice everything looks. That's about as much as they could expect from him.

The same is true of the house.

What would happen, say, if he never helped at all? The house would carry on as normal. The guests would manage on their own. They wouldn't need a host; they would host themselves.

With minimal input on his behalf, Bevan Breakfast is doing well. It has been a success, hasn't it? It would be too much to call it a social triumph. But even so, it has been a marketing success.

The sound of the doorbell allows him to stop thinking about the house, and to think instead, with some regret, about walking downstairs.

You can hear someone opening the front door.

Hello, someone says.

It sounds like Daryl, but this would be odd. It's unusual for Daryl to talk to strangers, who he usually regards with suspicion.

Daryl is calling up the stairs, 'Someone's at the door.'

The first thought is to hurry along. Daryl is greeting someone, which is a disaster. He almost wonders whether he should run downstairs, just to stop any damage that could occur.

It would all make sense if they were expecting a guest. No-one is due to arrive, though.

Then the thought suddenly occurs to him.

It might be Muriel!

If so, there has been no time to prepare. He had better pull on some socks. He had better pull on a clean shirt. If she is going to see him like this, he would rather she didn't see him at all. To see him like this would not leave the desired impression. If Muriel were to step inside his bedroom, he would probably jump from the balcony.

At the back of his mind is a list of things he is supposed to have done, all of which have a cross, rather than a tick, against them. All the things he would like to do – wash his body, for instance – cannot be done in time. He must check his face in the mirror. The key is to look unkempt rather than ill. Even if it's someone other than Muriel, the risk is not worth taking. It must be Muriel. Who else would come to see him?

On the short walk across the landing, he is able to button his shirt.

What put him on alert was the sound of the doorbell. It made him think about Muriel. It made him realise that he must stop being complacent.

Someone is coming up the stairs.

By the sound of the creaking floorboards, you can tell it's not Muriel. There is something distinctive about the pacing, too. There is a lumbering aspect.

He reaches for the banister and, looking down below, sees the famous balding crown of Barry Jack Thorne.

Aside from the balcony suicide, the only way he can think of responding is by locking himself in the toilet. Still, doing such a thing would be an insufficient match for his anger. This is Barry. This is the man who bloodied his nose. No, a punch in the face would be better. A punch on the nose would reflect his emotion.

Barry is standing below, wearing the look of a lumberjack with his hands stuck in his pockets. Barry, who hadn't called in advance, and hasn't left so much as an answering message in a month, opens his mouth and says, 'I want to apologise.'

'Why?'

'I shouldn't have hit you.'

Barry pulls open a rucksack from which he lifts a bottle of red wine.

'I've brought you something.'

The anger, which had been building, is beginning to fade. What stops him from throwing a punch is the wine bottle. You can't hit a man who is giving you a drink. Then it worries him that he was ever contemplating violence at all.

'I just came to say congratulations.'

'For what?'

'For what you've done.'

It takes a moment to understand that Barry is referring to the guesthouse.

'You've been on the news,' Barry says. 'I don't know how you've done it, mind. I thought I knew all the tricks of the trade.'

'There was no trick.'

'Don't be modest.'

There is no reason why Barry should continue his ascent. The bedroom will remain fortified.

Barry rubs his chin. 'Are we going to stand here all day?'

'What else would we do?'

'Come on. Let's see your bedroom.'

They might as well.

On balance, he would rather humour Barry than risk the alternative, which is to argue on the steps.

They enter the bedroom.

You can tell Barry is concerned by the lack of mess. There is no justification for the cleanliness. Things have gotten bad so it was only natural that he should clean. It's something to do. You would hope that things might degenerate a little more.

If he ever had the opportunity to dismiss Barry, it has certainly passed.

'Nice view,' Barry says, stepping onto the balcony. 'What are they doing?'

'Rehearsing a play.'

Barry laughs, as if rehearsing a play is the weirdest thing you could ever do.

It's a good thing none of the actors can see them. They are consumed in the art.

Barry looks across and says, 'I spoke to your wife the other day.'

There is no equivalent of a double take for words. You could say pardon, but it's not the same as a double take.

What Barry said didn't sound real. It sounded like it belonged to another world. Sometimes you wonder whether Muriel ever speaks to anyone.

'She was shopping for groceries,' Barry says. 'It was just starting to rain, so we didn't talk long.'

'What did you talk about?'

'I introduced myself.'

'And?'

'She knew who I was.'

'Great.'

'I mentioned this place, which she knew all about. She said your daughter told her.'

'Do you think she might visit?'

'I doubt it. She's got a dog.'

'A dog?'

'Yeah. A whippet.'

'We don't own a dog.'

'She got it last week.'

'What's the dog called?'

'Bruno.'

A dog in his own home. In their thirty-one years of marriage, they had never talked about getting a dog. Muriel had mentioned it for a brief while, maybe, but never in a serious way. It never seemed practical. They never had enough time for a Bruno.

'She said she was working on something,' Barry says.

'On what?'

'I don't know. She just said she was always up late, working on something. What is she, a painter?'

'A photographer.'

'That's it.'

Down below there is laughter. The actors are laughing. George must have said something funny.

Barry steps onto the carpet. 'I think you should go and see her,' he says.

'She can visit me.'

'You're naïve, then.'

'What am I supposed to do? Take a lie detector test?'

'That might work.'

'It makes no sense.'

'That's the thing with women,' Barry says. 'They move on.'

There is nothing to say, so Barry continues. 'Do you want to see her?'

'That's not the point.'

'I could drive you.'

'No thanks.'

No matter how awful things might become, the thought of sitting in a car next to Barry, for several hours, is difficult to accept. There is no scenario he can envisage where he would wish to do such a thing.

'Well, you think about it,' Barry says. 'I won't be leaving until Wednesday. I'm meeting a client in Hanger Lane. Remember that hotel?'

'You like it there.'

Barry lifts the rucksack and says, 'You know me, Street. I don't have any opinions on anything.'

It's true, actually. Barry doesn't have any opinions. Barry just likes to be a nuisance.

They don't have much else to say.

Barry offers his hand, as if to complete a successful

business deal. 'I better get going.'

'Well, thanks for the wine.'

'Pleasure.'

This is the moment they were supposed to be fighting. What happened to the anger? It was wrong to think he would punch Barry on the nose, or lock himself in the toilet.

'And once again, well done mate. I'm proud of you.'

'Thanks, Barry.'

It feels strange to receive this kind of praise, when he doesn't feel like a victor. There is nothing to celebrate.

The way in which Barry closes the door is more gentle than he expected.

It was nice of Barry to bring the wine, but knowing Barry, there will be some motive behind it. It wouldn't be a surprise if Barry wanted some money to invest in a travelling circus, or a leper colony. It could be anything.

Then he closes the curtains so he doesn't have to look outside. He can get back to whatever he was doing. Yes, he will change the bed linen, so that he might sleep better tonight. He would rather spend his evening here, under the covers, than anywhere else.

Then he finds himself changing the bed sheets, conscious now, more than ever, that he is alone. He is conscious of nothing else, except that he is awake, and that it's wrong to be awake. What is standing here going to achieve? It would be better to fall asleep, but he isn't able to do so. Sleep is beyond his potential.

There is a voice in his head that belongs to Muriel.

The voice says, 'You're still a bastard.'

Then he pulls the covers over his body and the first thing that comes to his mind is that fucking dog.

Sixteen

'It's not just a guesthouse,' he says, which is how it begins. 'You should think of it as a system.'

'A system?'

'A way to live.'

It's not clear what he means by this. It made sense in the moment, just before the words left his mouth. It has been repeated in his mind so many times that he's almost forgotten what it means.

'I don't know what I mean, exactly. But I know I want to live for a reason.'

'And you think you've found one?'

'I think so.'

Then he explains, with a more careful choice of words, that he wants to use his time on this earth to do something useful.

'I have an expiry date. In a few years, no-one is going to eat me.'

It's only the sight of the tape recorder, which he had almost forgotten about, that brings his thought to an end.

There is a purpose to the guesthouse, which is imprecise but important, if only he could say what it is. There is a philosophy, and he is loath to say spirit, but what else can you call it?

'I just remember being a child, and how everyone used to say it's important to share,' he continues. 'And seeing as Rosalind has a big house, I thought we could make something of it.'

'A commune?'

'I don't want to call it that. A micro society, you could call it.'

There is no reason to feel ashamed for talking like this. What we gain in pretentiousness, we also gain in accuracy. The language behind the thing is unimportant. It's the thing itself that counts.

Then he mentions how sharing, as a formal way to live, should not be consigned to the world of children.

'It's not just about homeless people either. We'll provide a sanctuary for everyone. I want to see bankers and lawyers coming here, working together and painting.'

'They'd love that.'

He wants to say *they'll love what I tell them to love,* but decides, sensibly, to avoid saying this. It wouldn't reflect well on the project. It would highlight a central problem, too. How can you stop someone from being a moron if that's what they're determined to be? It's no good to say, *it should be a home for morons as well.* The morons might not want salvation. What do morons want? Has he ever thought to ask them?

Then it makes him wonder if he's only ranting to himself, when really he should be communicating with people; after all, people are the subject, the exhibit, and focus.

There is a pigeon walking towards them with a kind of head butt action.

It was better to meet in the wooded clearing, in the sun, than to speak on the telephone. The trunk is a good spot. The tyre swing and sparrows and whatever else allow you to forget there is chaos in the world.

'I want to help Rosalind, as well.'

'Help how?'

'To give her a platform.'

Then he explains that although the art itself is beyond his comprehension, he can see its value in a therapeutic sense.

'It's how she expresses herself.'

'Is that the same for your wife?'

'Yes, Muriel too,' he says, although this is something to mourn, rather than celebrate.

It's a credit to Gideon that he can listen, as a journalist-cum-therapist, without making a brutal comment. It's not an interview so much as a therapy session.

'I wonder,' Gideon says. 'What have you done with your party membership card?'

'It's in a landfill site.'

'You don't feel like you belong to the party?'

'I don't like parties.'

It's better to avoid these questions. It's better to focus on the project. If he were to discuss his political history, it would sound like he was talking about someone else. He could discuss dialectical materialism, or the riots of 1968, but it would sound like he was talking about a fossil.

There comes a point, not long after, when the presence of the tape recorder seems unimportant. This is the moment of liberation. This is the point at which he could say anything he likes and not feel inhibited.

'Who's the source, then?'

Gideon withdraws the tape recorder and presses the stop button. It's a shame that a journalist should have to burden himself by telling the truth.

'I'm still working on it,' Gideon says.

'I want to know.'

'I'm meeting the editor next week.'

'Well, I hope he tells the truth.'

'So do I.'

There is nothing left to say.

The pigeon has flown.

Seventeen

There is a kind of anticipation about what we are to witness, which is a play, about forty minutes in length, and which Rosalind and George have worked on together. It's a credit to both of them, in fact, that the kitchen is beginning to fill with lots of strangers. It's better to be sceptical rather than hostile about it all.

The crowd are older than what we have seen so far. Some of them have brought their adult children. Some of them are wearing sweaters with shirts underneath. At least two of the women have had cosmetic surgery, which is not a slight against them, but rather, something to notice.

The guests have come so frequently that he hasn't had time to think about who they are. He thinks of them in a crude, lazy way by their nationalities, because he doesn't have the energy to know them by anything else. He doesn't have much contact, except for the brief conversations on the landing, or during the exchange of money. It's easier for Rosalind and George, who spend long nights with the guests getting drunk at the kitchen table.

The aim is to reach the fridge without speaking to anyone. In reality, he must shake their hands and smile as much as he can. Let them say what a brilliant man he is. He can smile and say something to the effect of yes, I am brilliant.

What culture have these people bought into? Perhaps they belong to no defined group. Perhaps it is he who is lost. Where does he belong? No-one has invented a category for him. He would like one, though. He would like a category. He would like to belong to something.

It must have been a good night, judging by the crushed beer cans in the recycling box. From the side he lifts a plate on which there is a wooden knife and wooden fork. With the metal tongs he grabs a hunk of salad.

At the table he has noticed, but not acted upon, the presence of George senior. In his baseball cap, George senior is like an industrialist who wants to ingratiate himself to his peasant following. This is an exaggeration, of course, but the potential is there.

The Germans, to his satisfaction, are talking - laughing, in fact. George senior is telling them a story. One of the women, whose name he had forgotten almost as soon as she arrived, is laughing so much that she can't even lift a fork to her mouth.

George senior puts on a Geordie accent, saying coo as you would say cow.

And the youngest says, 'Coo!'

All of them are laughing.

What convinced him to come downstairs was the prospect of food, and some hope that the occasion might attract a calmer crowd. It was about five seconds after entering the kitchen that the hope was extinguished.

Then he reaches out a hand so that George senior can clasp it.

'Let me shake your hand,' George senior says.

It had never occurred to him that George senior would talk like this. Warmth was not a word he would have associated with the man.

They could talk for longer, but you get the impression they would talk about nothing except the house. He has done enough talking about Bevan Breakfast.

'I'm impressed by the artwork,' George senior says. 'It's absolutely first class. I said to Rosalind, this is absolutely first class.'

'Good.'

'You've done a tremendous job.'

'Thanks, George.'

When you go through the list of everything that's happened, it seems odd to think he should take any credit at all. George has done the marketing; Rosalind has done the art. What does he bring? The face, maybe. The face is what matters.

Then he finds himself wandering to the sink without really having ended the conversation. In a formal sense, the conversation never came to an end.

Despite the praise and the column inches, nothing could have prepared him for the sorts of things people are saying. It's incredible, Joe. The energy is amazing. When are you getting back into politics? You should write a book about it.

There are two things happening. Most of the people are having conversations in his outer presence. The second thing is the food, which is being prepared by Daryl, and for the moment, Rosalind. The kitchen has two moods: one of work, and one of leisure. It's a schizophrenic kitchen.

Rosalind is removing a tray from the oven. She is wearing oven gloves. This doesn't seem right, somehow. Ordinarily, she would only wear oven gloves if she were handling something toxic.

It was sensible to walk here so that he could free himself from the laws of conversation. Now that he can see Rosalind, it seems sensible, as well, to make some kind of gesture.

'Can I do something?'

'Everything's done,' Rosalind says.

She says the best way he can help is to talk to people. That's what he ought to do.

'But I want to do something.'

'Then talk to them.'

What he actually wanted was for her to say yes, you can peel some carrots. The problem is that there are many hours of talk to endure. The play won't last long, but the conversations will continue until the night has passed. He might as well get drunk.

*

'Don't let it slip,' George says.

George and Daryl are holding the armchair at both ends. To an outsider, there must be something comical about their struggle. Everyone on the patio knows better. The armchair is for the purposes of drama.

Some of the guests are applauding the armchair, as if it were the Olympic torch coming down the Mall. George is giving Daryl instructions on where to position his feet. The armchair is heading to the garden. You'd have thought they might have planned this further in advance, but the spirit of the house wouldn't allow for such a thing.

The amphitheatre – if you can call it that – was prepared this morning. The action will happen on the lawn, which is large enough. On the slope towards the lawn is a rug on which the young adults are sitting. A young woman is smoking, and holding a glass of wine. It must be nice to get drunk and watch a play.

On the patio are four rows of lightweight folding chairs.

With his chair under his arm, he decides to walk to the back row, where nobody will see him. He positions his chair at the back of the patio. He would rather watch from the balcony, but to do so would be rude.

No doubt the play will ask probing questions, such as how to survive in a world you don't recognise as your own. It might ask no such question. Does it matter? No, he should just try to watch. He owes this much to Rosalind. He should try to focus. Concentration is something difficult. It's not easy to concentrate when you feel no obvious compulsion to do so. Besides, his opinion counts for nothing. If it should matter at all, it should matter in terms of blind support, and to indulge his sense of what a father should be. Should his opinion matter for any artistic reason? He could give some advice, but it would be worthless, and people might laugh at him for doing so.

The ritual doesn't need to be explained to him. However terrible the performance, his duty must be to express his fondness for all the actors involved. Their display, however bad it may turn out, must become, in the after-show at least, an unqualified triumph.

He is not aware that anything is about to happen until the spectators put their hands together. It spreads from front to back, until he finds himself clapping.

The opening scene is of a domestic kitchen table. He recognises the table, which belongs in the living room of the house. There is a yellow chrysanthemum in a vase. Further back in the garden is the washing line, which is supposed to evoke a back yard.

The first person to emerge is a young lad whose age will be what, twenty-one? The main thing you notice is the speed at which the boy walks. It's difficult to know whether the actor himself came in a grey woollen shirt, or whether it's part of the costume. It would look more natural in an art class. The lad probably smells of incense.

The lad positions himself at the table.

You can tell something is wrong. Something bad has happened.

Someone else emerges - this time a middle-aged man with a beard. Not a deliberate beard, but the kind that suggests he hasn't been thinking straight. This must be the father. It would seem like a reasonable assumption to make.

'Where is she?' the father says.

These are the first words of the play.

The lad looks up from the table and says, 'She must have jumped a wall.'

'They're looking, aren't they?'

'Yeah.'

'What did they tell you?'

'They said they're looking, Dad.'

The father is silent, pressing his finger on his chin.

There is no clue as to what we should be thinking. What do

we know? We know that someone is lost. We know that she escaped by jumping a wall. We know that people are looking.

The most extraordinary thing is the father, who doesn't know what to do. The father is standing with his fists clenched and looks ready to punch something.

In the yard is the actress. You can see she is waiting. She enters without looking at anyone, and without giving a clue as to what she's thinking. You get the impression she must have been looking around outside.

'I give up,' she says.

Short, blonde and with the familiar voice from rehearsals, she moves towards the table and pulls out a chair. She is wearing a big grey jumper. The sleeves reach the edge of her knuckles. Her nails will be dirty. She is leaning on the table, with her hair covering her eyes. We can hardly see her face. It's hard to tell what she's thinking.

She is positioned just opposite the young man. The two of them, most probably, are brother and sister. The lad puts an arm around her shoulder. There is something quite simple and profound about the sight. It's something you should see more often from brothers and sisters.

The father, in his brown shirt, is unable to sit down. We are invited to look at him and think about how he arrived at this point. We are told what the time is – gone midnight – and we remember that someone is missing.

There follows a conversation in which the father talks about family and the importance of sticking together.

'Your mother's having trouble,' the father says, which means the mother must be missing. 'Right now she needs our support.'

There is a pause in which neither sibling seems to know what to say. Instead, the father continues.

'She'll come back. If there's a God in this universe she'll be alive. She will be.'

The father, when he said the words, managed to sound like a human being. It could have gone badly, with a line like that, but the result was a good one.

The play is not so bad. It was obvious within the first thirty seconds that it wouldn't be so bad. It offers something more than expected. It's possible to recognise this imagined world, which doesn't seem as sentimental as it might. You can tell the acting is first-rate because you almost forget you're watching a piece of drama. It's only on the odd occasion, like now, that the conceit begins to slip.

The most interesting person to watch is the father, who doesn't know how to keep still.

'We all love each other,' the father says. 'We'll be alright. Won't we?'

And the son says yeah, which is all the son needed to say.

The daughter motions with her hand that she might wish to say something.

'It's not about whether we love each other,' she says. 'It's about whether she felt our love.'

'What do you mean?' the father says.

The daughter begins to tell a story in which we find out the mother had been attending therapy for years. She had been seeing a psychiatrist more recently and began a course of medication.

'How could we have stopped any of that?' the father says.

'Perhaps we couldn't,' the daughter says. 'But you could have been more supportive.'

'How?'

'When she was in therapy, I mean.'

'I was there.'

'You thought the whole thing was a waste of time.'

'It was a waste of time. They can't tell you anything you don't already know.'

'So what should we have told her?'

'To snap out of it.'

There is silence, which is the fault of the father, and nothing to do with the children. To some extent, the father is culpable for the problems of his wife. A lack of love, you could call it.

After this outburst, the brother and sister look at one another.

'Come on, Dad,' the lad says.

'What?'

From this point in the play, the emphasis becomes more to do with the father, his guilt, and how to overcome it. The sadness of his wife is the consequence, in part, of his disdain for therapy. She needed help and he gave nothing but scorn.

The siblings continue to follow this line of attack, which feels like a process of rehabilitation, as much as anything.

The father, for his part, is eager to make a case for his integrity.

'You're all responsible, just as much as I am,' the father says. 'You're all up to your neck in it.'

'Hardly,' the daughter says.

'You talk like I'm the only one with any explaining to do.'

'You are.'

'She was getting better before you got involved.'

'What does that mean?'

'It was the shopping.'

'What?'

'If there's one thing that could have pushed her over the edge it was the shopping.'

'What the hell has shopping got to do with it?'

'She used to hate shopping. She never used to worry about what she was wearing and what she looked like. You got her obsessed.'

'I was the only one who took her out. She felt good about herself.'

'Why was she depressed, then?'

'It wasn't the ballet pumps we bought, if that's what you're thinking.'

'Stop acting like I'm being unreasonable.'

'You are.'

The son is holding his mouth, doing his best to cover his smile. The father and daughter look at the lad. You know what's coming next.

'What's funny?' the father says.

'Nothing.'

'Come on. We're a family. We share things.'

'You two make me laugh. That's all.'

'I don't think there's anything to laugh about.'

There is a sense that all three of them are beginning to move apart. Things are beginning to worsen.

'As if you're in a position to laugh,' says the sister, or daughter. 'When did you ever spend time with mum?'

'I did my share.'

'You were too busy getting drunk.'

'I've got a life, haven't I?' the lad says, which is to imply that his sister doesn't.

Then, just as you would expect, the lad says there was nothing wrong with his actions. There was nothing wrong with going out and drinking. That's what young people do. You wouldn't want to spoil his fun, would you?

'Grow up,' she says.

'I'll do what I want.'

'You should grow up.'

'Do you honestly think Mum gives a shit?'

To the son, the health of his mother is important, no doubt, but it has to compete with the other aspects of his life. It's hard to balance everything at once. Some people, like George senior, would call the boy a lazy, feckless layabout. This would be unfair. There is more to the kid than this. There is a fundamental kindness to the boy, even if he lets his family down. You get the impression that at the age of twenty-one or so, the boy doesn't quite know what he wants to be. Youth is supposed to be a time of excitement. It's not working out that way.

Then his sister turns around and says, 'Do you ever tell Mum you love her?'

'Stop asking these stupid questions.'

'It's not a stupid question.'

'Everything you've said has been stupid.'

It's remarkable to think this is the same brother and sister that were almost hugging just a while ago. The siblings aren't so cuddly anymore.

'Come on,' the father says. 'Do you think your mother wants you to argue like this?'

In truth, none of them seem to know what the mother would want. It doesn't seem to be clear to anyone.

There is a period of calm, in which you wonder whether they will ever raise their voices again. They talk about childhood memories, and some of the funny things the mother used to say. She used to talk in her sleep, they remember, which allows them to laugh. There was a time when she would only buy salad pots from Sainsbury's, and never make her own. She didn't trust herself to make a good salad. And the lad remembers how she once left a twenty-pound note under his pillow because she didn't have any change for the tooth fairy.

There is laughter. There is real laughter among the three of them. You would hope they might stand a chance of being a family again.

It's only by listening that you can understand the truth at the heart of the play. Nobody has taken responsibility. The father hasn't done enough to love his wife. The siblings, too, have underestimated how much love their mother may require. The truth is that nobody has loved her enough. It doesn't seem likely that things will change. There won't be an end to it.

The play must end somehow.

The audience have perfected their silence.

George and Rosalind have created something harrowing, which could only be considered a good thing in the company they consort with.

Before anything else is said, there is a figure emerging from the side.

She is pale, middle-aged, and most probably, the mother. She is wearing a tiara, with a white dress in her arms. If she looks to have escaped from anywhere, it seems to have been a wedding.

The lad rushes forward and says, 'Mum?'

'What are you wearing?' the daughter says.

She doesn't look at her children; she continues to walk, almost with a limp.

She pulls down a bottle from the cabinet. She unscrews the lid. From the drawer she pulls out a packet of tablets. She empties the tablets onto her palm. She leans back and takes a swig, allowing herself to grimace.

'Oh,' she says, positioning herself at the table. 'Tell me something.'

The father is watching from a distance.

'What?'

The mother pulls the yellow chrysanthemum from the vase.

She clenches it.

Then she looks up and says, 'Am I alive or am I dead?'

That will be the payoff.

We see the father looking at his son and daughter.

There is nothing to say.

We are left with a view of the mother. The only thing she can do is slump her head on the table. This is how the play ends.

Has it really ended? Of course it has because the audience begin to applaud. The show is over. We can see that the father is just an actor, among other actors. The mother too, is transformed into the woman she was before.

Rosalind and George are pulled to the front. The cheer from the crowd is louder than anything that came before. There is a bouquet for Rosalind and a bottle of champagne for George. The two of them are smiling at each other. Someone from the crowd shouts, 'Speech!'

We can hear George, who says thank you, and thank you very much. The first thing George says is to praise the actors, which brings another round of applause. When George mentions the play, it's obvious that the rest of the speech will come naturally. It has been the culmination of several weeks of hard work. Special thanks must go to Rosalind, without whom none of this would be possible.

Rosalind too, is able to commend her creative partner, and make a joke about the hours spent in her hooded jumper and pyjamas.

There is another round of applause.

Here they come, ascending the steps to the patio like a victorious cup final team. It would be advisable to stand aside so the actors can pass. It takes a moment for Rosalind to disentangle herself from the hugs.

Between him and Rosalind is a crowd of strangers. He must tell Rosalind what a pleasure it was, and how proud it made him feel to watch the play. It would be inaccurate to give any other opinion.

Rosalind is coming closer but the path between them is riddled with idiots. Just when it looks like Rosalind will say hello there is an idiot in front of him, and then another. The race is to congratulate Rosalind. The starting gun went over his head.

The only solution is to stand and wait a minute longer. It would be rude to go upstairs. It's something he can imagine himself doing, though. If things get much worse he can imagine himself going to bed.

Really, he would like to stand somewhere else. There is only so much satisfaction you can get from watching other people smiling. Everyone is talking about the play. There is nothing else to talk about.

If he thinks about the content, a problem will arise. It will force him to confront the ideas. What motivated Rosalind to get involved in such a thing? What were her artistic reasons? It's not possible to get an answer because Rosalind is talking to someone else.

What surprises him is how close George is standing behind Rosalind. The two of them are having separate conversations, but you get the sense they are waiting for each other. In between some of the words, George looks at Rosalind, who returns the glance, as if to say she will be with him in a minute.

Why was it important for George to write the play?

The themes are easy to identify. Guilt is one of them. All of the family have neglected to love their mother as much as they might have done. The result has been a family disaster, even if the ending was open to interpretation. But how does this relate to George? If anything, it makes him think of his own life. And he thinks about whether it's possible that he might have neglected Muriel.

The play was supposed to make him forget about things. Somehow, it has made him think too much. This was never the intention, but this was the result. Should he stop worrying about fictional characters and focus on the real ones? It might be best to stop thinking.

Eighteen

The intention was to fortify his bedroom, and this has been a success. No-one will attempt to bridge it. The fort has a perimeter. It has an invisible line at the top of the landing. The territory includes the bathroom. Nowhere else is necessary.

It would be a mistake to get up and do something. On the odd occasion, it might be permissible to ring for a pizza, and venture into the hall. It would be better if the mattress could grow wings. He could fly somewhere.

It would be good if he had a gong next to him. If he hit the gong then Rosalind would come for him.

There is no rush to do anything. There is no need to wash, despite his smell, and the hours spent in bed. He could lie here until summer.

The light from the window says that it's daytime. No matter how tight the curtains are closed, the light is able to seep through. It would be better to tape a black bin bag across the window.

It has been a while since he looked in a mirror. He knows that his skin is pale, but not so pale as to cause alarm. His hair has been flattened by days spent on a pillow. His body is wrapped in the duvet. A cocoon! A cocoon is what he needed. He ought to tell Rosalind that he has found a cocoon.

Someone is coming closer. Just by listening to the footsteps, it's likely to be Rosalind. What are the odds that she will call a doctor? The longer he lies here, the further the odds will shorten. This would be the worst thing to happen.

Rosalind opens the door.

She doesn't look angry. If anything, she has no idea what to say.

'When are you coming down?'

'I don't know.'

'You're missing everything.'

Then she steps closer and places down a cup of tea. Were it not for the tea, it would be unacceptable for her to bridge the fort.

She reaches out a hand and says, 'Why are you upset?'

'I'm not. I'm just having a moment.'

'A moment?'

'Yes.'

She is not going to leave the room.

He does the wrong thing, which is to look at the wall. And yet she doesn't look angry. Something else is allowed to dominate. It's concern, if anything.

She looks at the curtains as if he is mad to have kept them closed. If she had her way, she would vacuum the floor and dust the walls. And she hates cleaning.

She puts a hand on the bed when she says, 'Do you miss Mum?'

'I don't know about that.'

'You do miss her,' she says. 'Otherwise you wouldn't be having a moment.'

This is probably true.

He is disturbed by his own thoughts, and the truth in what Rosalind says. The thought that Muriel might visit is beginning to feel more remote. All he can tell is that for some reason, Muriel will continue to ignore him. To see Muriel would be an accomplishment. Really, he should think of her as a person, rather than a mountain he has to climb.

'She hates me.'

'No, I wouldn't say that.'

'Then what?'

'She hates what you did to her,' Rosalind says. 'She knows

the Helen thing was bullshit, though.'

'But she never said anything.'

'Well, you can't erase the things you actually did.'

'No, but… '

'And if a guy cheated on me,' she says, and then she pauses.

Then, as if to recognise and dismiss the memory in the same moment, she allows herself to smile. You can tell she is more relaxed, and happier, than when he first came to the house.

At the door she says that he should come downstairs.

'We miss you,' she says.

She holds the stare for long enough.

Then she closes the door.

It's a relief that he should be left alone.

*

'Look at the state of you,' Barry says the next morning. 'You look like shit.'

'Thanks.'

'Have you washed?'

'No.'

'Someone ought to wash you.'

The whole thing is embarrasing.

Whoever let Barry inside has done the house a great disservice.

He should have remembered it was Wednesday, which is when Barry said he was driving home. He should have known that Barry would come back. In fact, he should have instructed Rosalind to turn Barry away. She could have said he was ill. It wouldn't have been too much of a lie, would it? There would have been an element of truth.

'Are you coming then?'

'I don't want to go anywhere.'

'I'm giving you a lift, Joe.'

Then Barry says he can wait twenty minutes, so there is no

rush at all. There is plenty of time to pack a suitcase.

'But I don't want to go.'

'You'll feel better on the journey,' Barry says.

Barry looks around for something to do. It's admirable that Barry should attempt to sidestep the underpants on the floor.

'It's dark in here,' Barry says. 'Do you want me to open the curtains?'

'No.'

Barry lifts the jeans and belt from the pile. This is a good reason to protest.

'What are you doing?'

'I'm picking up your clothes.'

'Please stop.'

This is too much. The fort has been bridged.

The first obstacle to get past is Barry.

He begins to walk, bringing the duvet, which is the same thing as bringing the cocoon.

It seemed so likely that nothing could drag him from the bedroom. Nothing, not even a disaster like Barry, could drag him away. But to stay in bed would be impossible.

'Where are you going?' Barry says.

'Somewhere else.'

What was the plan? If the plan were written down it would be easy to remember. The plan was to get away, wasn't it? How can you get away when the past keeps chasing you down? Oh, what a despicable man you are, Barry Thorne!

In his cocoon, he tiptoes down the first step, and then the second.

Despite his eagerness to bring the cocoon, he is able to walk at a good pace.

The further he walks, the quicker the pace becomes.

Barry is following but there is enough distance between them to feel like he could escape if he wanted. Where would he go? That will be decided soon. It might be that Barry decides to leave him alone. It might be that he is able to stay, after all. The fort could be rebuilt. It has incurred structural damage, that's all.

Over his shoulder he can hear Barry, who is breathing hard, almost like a dog. It seems to require a massive effort for Barry to bring his stomach with him. It's impossible for Barry to rush and shout at the same time. This is the nice thing.

When Rosalind sees him in the hall, the first thing she does is smile.

'Oh good,' she says.

Through his eyes, he gives an indication that it's wrong to say, oh good. Nothing is good.

'What's wrong?'

Then it occurs to him that he doesn't have anything to say.

Nothing is wrong, as such. He just wanted some peace. He wanted to be left alone.

Barry is standing a safe distance, with a hand on his chest.

'I was saying to Joe that he should come with me.'

'That's a good idea,' Rosalind says.

Rosalind says it would be a good chance to see Muriel. If anything, she says, it would be wise to get out of the house.

'But she doesn't want to see me.'

'All you can do is try.'

She is like a mother telling a child that his first day of school will be alright. That's how it feels.

Barry is nodding. Barry would have liked to say what Rosalind said. Barry lacks the words. What a shame that Barry should be seen as a normal person. It shouldn't be possible.

Rosalind is thinking. There is an important issue at hand. If she thought it was trivial, she would have left the room.

'You can bring back some of your stuff,' she says. 'Your books, your clothes.'

It feels like there are too many carrots being dangled in front of him. Neither Barry nor Rosalind will be happy until he's on the road. Rosalind is concerned for his wellbeing. She is eager that he returns to his normal state. With Barry, of course, there will always be a motive. Just to hazard a guess, there is a vague chance that Barry will ask him to front a radio show, or do an interview. There are plenty of things Barry would like him to do. There are plenty of column inches that can be written, all of which can be filled by the lies and distortions of Thorne Associates.

If, as Barry suggests, they would simply drive north, see Muriel, then return within a couple of nights, there is no harm to be done. He can resist whatever motive Barry may have. It wouldn't matter so much.

'Fine, I'll come.'

'Nice one,' Barry says.

Rosalind is smiling, which is a good thing, of course.

There is no fanfare. There is no sudden change in their act. They make it seem like his decision was a formality, when really he agonised over it.

Then he feels conscious that he must look stupid in his cocoon, which is actually a duvet. It was stupid to think he could sleep forever. The fort wasn't built to last. It served a purpose, which was to protect him for a while. The lesson is that you can't escape from anything. It doesn't matter what you do. Should he apologise? He owes Rosalind an apology for making her worry. He owes Barry nothing.

'I'm sorry.'

'It's alright,' Barry says.

'I was talking to Rosalind.'

It's time to say goodbye. It might not be goodbye forever, but he must go.

He pulls the raincoat from the hook.

'I'll help you pack,' Rosalind says.

Things are beginning to happen all at once.

It doesn't seem real that he might see Muriel. It's something to be excited about, isn't it? The trouble is that he hadn't thought about what to do with this moment. The moment was always likely to come, but he hadn't thought about it.

'Thank you.'

He kisses his daughter on the cheek.

*

On the journey, along the M1 for the most part, there is nothing much to see. They pass through what is sometimes called the lungs of London. They dissect it without catching a glimpse of its beauty, assuming it exists. Nothing is beautiful when you can only see bridges, service stations and miles of arable farmland. In the south of England, you have to travel quite deep into the countryside to find something beautiful.

He is sitting in the passenger seat, wrapped in his cocoon. Just beneath his feet is a cereal box. On the dashboard is a furry cotton ball with goggle eyes. You would think the objects were placed here by some kind of disturbed person. It's only when you look around that some of the ordinary things come into view. In the storage compartment are some betting slips. There is a tray of grapes on the backseat, most of which have been eaten.

He is allowed his choice of radio – Five Live – which is suitably dull and neutral.

On the hour is the summary of the news.

The broadcaster says something about the inevitability of war.

'Do you mind if I change it?'

'Go ahead,' Barry says.

On the next station there is music, which is loud, and causes him to lower the volume.

Barry is looking at the road and says, 'She'll be pleased to see you.'

'She doesn't know I'm coming.'

'Did you not want to tell her?'

'I like to do things unannounced.'

The way in which Barry manages the situation is to remain silent, and look ahead at the road.

'She must have missed you.'

There is no reason to answer.

'Come on,' Barry says. 'Don't you think so?'

'I don't think so.'

There is silence.

'What are you going to say to her?'

'I'll see if we can start again.'

'Right.'

'Or maybe we'll go away somewhere.'

'That'd be nice.'

'Or maybe we could live with Rosalind and pretend to be a family.'

He must continue to speak. There is a danger that Barry will take control.

'I just want to know she's okay.'

'Of course.'

'I haven't heard from her at all, you see.'

'I know.'

'So it might be awkward.'

Barry turns for a moment and says, 'She was probably waiting for you to bite the bullet.'

'Well, that's what I'm doing.'

There is a road sign that predicts another two hundred and twenty miles to go. This is disappointing.

Some of the place names have been excellent. Leighton Buzzard was the best.

'It'll be late by the time we get there,' Barry says. 'Why don't you come back to ours?'

'Really?'

'There's plenty of room on the floor.'

'Thanks. I'll be alright.'

'You can shower in the morning and sort yourself out. If you don't mind me saying, you look like shit, mate.'

'Cheers.'

'I just think you should get a good night's sleep before seeing her. You don't want her to see you like this.'

'Like what?'

'Like shit.'

There is plenty more to come. There is another three hours

of this.

Already, his legs are beginning to stiffen.

Then Barry talks at great length, and without justification, about his new laminate flooring.

'I only got it done last week,' Barry says. 'You can be the first to try it out.'

Does this mean he will be the first to step on it, or the first to sleep on it? Nothing is certain.

Then, without realising how it happened, the conversation moves onto the subject of love. Barry starts some of his sentences with words like, 'what women want,' as if three billion people who happen to share the same chromosome would all want the same thing. If we accept Barry's logic, love is just a way of tricking someone into caring about you. This is an awful way in which to view the world. Then it makes him wonder how Barry ever got to middle age without growing up.

'I'll tell you something,' Barry says. 'I used to get up to all sorts. And I mean all sorts.'

'Like?'

Barry smiles at whatever memory is in his head. 'I used to visit a woman.'

'A prostitute?'

'No,' Barry says. 'Why do you say that?'

'Carry on.'

'She wasn't your typical sort of woman.'

In his mind he thinks *transsexual*, but he doesn't want to say it.

'She was nice,' Barry says. 'But she went above and beyond what might be expected.'

'In what sense?'

Barry looks straight ahead. 'She used to hit me.'

'Hit you?'

'Quite badly.'

There is something exciting about what Barry has said. He would like to know more.

'How did you meet?'

'She was a client of mine. Then I became a client of hers.'

'How old was she?'

'She was older than me.'

'By how much?'

Barry looks at his hands, which are on the wheel. Barry is driving, of course, which means he can't count with his fingers.

'She was in her sixties.'

There is no particular way in which he can reply. It would be better to think of a question.

'How bad did it get?'

'Oh, it was terrible,' Barry says. 'It was like an addiction.'

Then Barry says a number of things that, in any context, would be deserving of ridicule.

'It was like dog training,' Barry says. 'As far as she was concerned, I was a dog.'

In the context of the car, with its cramped interior, it's better to remain silent.

'I used to walk around with thirty-foot of rope in my bag,' Barry says. 'Then my wife opened the bag one night and saw it. I had to tell her, of course.'

A cruel thought comes into his head.

'What did you tell her?'

He knows, of course, what Barry told her. He just wants Barry to say it aloud.

'That I was seeing a dominatrix.'

There is silence for a moment.

Then Barry says that his marriage recovered, against the odds, because it made him appreciate what he almost lost.

'Sarah was great about it,' Barry says. 'She was sad, of course, and I slept on the couch for a while, but she overcame it and said, 'Barry, I still want to make things work'.'

'That's good.'

'She said that some things happen for a reason.'

'Right.'

Barry explains that his wife is superstitious. She collects

tarot cards, and plays on Ouija boards. She believes in everything so long as it hasn't been proven. The more Barry describes his wife, the more she sounds like a bloody fool.

Then he feels himself getting tired, and wonders whether it would be rude to sleep. The advantage, of course, is that he could miss any PR proposals made by Barry. He could sleep through it all. It has been a decent ride, and there has been no mention of any ulterior motive.

'I won't lie to you,' Barry says. 'There are times when I feel guilty for what I did.'

Should he say something? A noise of acknowledgement would be the appropriate thing.

'Hmm.'

'I sometimes wonder whether I deserve her at all.'

There is something touching about this, or at least there would be had he not allowed such a bad image of Barry's wife to solidify in his mind.

'I can see what you did, with the guesthouse,' Barry says. 'I can see how it made you feel better.'

'What do you mean?'

'You've medicated yourself. It's like therapy, or something.'

'That wasn't the reason.'

'I know what it's like.'

'Do you?'

'You felt bad.'

'About what?'

'I know what it's like, Joe.'

The more Barry says he knows what it's like, the more irritating it gets. Barry knows nothing. If you were to seek the counsel of any man, the last person you would think of would be Barry Thorne.

The only way out is to sleep. The conversation has put him in an irritable mood.

Between the two of them, and without saying anything, they negotiate a situation where silence dominates.

It hadn't struck him as being something to look forward

to, the journey. It was always going to be a challenge. It was never going to be fun to sit here and listen to Barry. What makes it tolerable is the goal at the end. It's not like he's going to visit a stranger. This is about Muriel. It's about seeing if she still hates him. She might have forgiven him; she might want to make things work. Everything might be okay. Whatever happens, he ought to know what his duties are. He would like to know where he fits, if he even fits at all.

*

It must be close to midnight when they arrive.

The darkness prevents him from seeing much at all.

It's an apartment block round the back of a motorway underpass.

Some of the ground floor windows are protected with iron bars.

There is a neat line of wheelie bins.

It's a neighbourhood that he doesn't know very well. In fact, it's on the opposite side of town to his home. You could walk here in about half an hour. He has driven through it and wondered who might live in the estate next to the motorway, but there has never been any reason to visit. Never has somewhere felt so well connected and so cut-off at the same time.

Barry reverses into a parking space and says, 'Home.'

It doesn't feel like home. It feels like a pit stop.

Despite the ache in his legs, he has enough strength to open the passenger door and stand upright.

The building is more attractive close-up than from a distance. It has a series of rectangular balconies, some of which have floral decorations.

Barry is fumbling for his house keys. Barry seems agitated about standing on the doorstep too long.

'The neighbours are friendly,' Barry says. 'Most of them.'

There is a cat watching from atop a fence. The cat watches

them enter through the yellow door.

The communal flooring is chipped, which, according to Barry, is due to ongoing maintenance works. The stairwell has the cold, worthless feel of a school changing room. It wouldn't really matter if your shoes were muddy.

They walk upstairs.

On the door to number 26 is a scrawled message that reads: *No junk mail.*

'Just whisper,' Barry says, turning the key in the lock.

Barry flicks a light in the hall.

Straight away, the apartment is more inviting than you would expect from the outside. There is a good amount of space for Barry and his wife.

There is a corridor through which he follows Barry.

In the living room, with the famous laminate flooring, Barry removes each cushion from the couch. Then Barry lays the cushions on the floor.

'This is how I slept when our marriage broke down,' Barry says. 'It's comfier than it looks.'

'Thanks for this.'

'No problem, mate.'

Then Barry walks to another room without mentioning anything.

The living room is an odd place. On the face of it, there is nothing about the room that has anything to do with Barry. It would be difficult for Barry to explain the model ships in the cabinet, for instance. It doesn't seem to have any connection.

Barry returns with a pillow.

There is something important to ask.

'What's with the boats?'

'My dad was a yachtsman,' Barry says. 'He liked to collect souvenirs.'

'That's nice.'

There is something bewildering about the whole experience. It doesn't seem normal that he should be standing in Barry's apartment talking about nautical things. The day was never meant to end like this. Something wrong happened, along the way.

The reason he looks in the mirror is to see if he's ill. Are his eyes bloodshot, or were they always like that? He is exhausted. Barry was right. It was a good idea to come round.

Barry announces that he ought to go to sleep.

'I'm meeting a client tomorrow morning,' Barry says. 'He allegedly had a romp in a petrol station.'

'I see.'

'He's a good lad, actually.'

Barry closes the curtains.

'Sleep well,' Barry says.

'And you.'

It won't take him long to unpack his things. First there is the toothbrush, then the nightshirt, and finally his alarm clock.

Then he looks at the floor and wonders what to do.

Should he make a plan?

No, there is nothing to plan.

In the morning he will wake up. He will have an opportunity to make things better.

Everything will be resolved.

It might be a good day.

Nineteen

'You don't believe in anything?'

'Nope.'

'Not even ghosts?'

He looks up from his mug of coffee and tells Mrs Thorne that no, he doesn't believe in ghosts.

'Oh, you're one of those people,' she says.

It's no surprise to discover that she's like this. Barry had mentioned his wife, which had prepared him for the worst.

The kitchen is too small to be shared with such a person. There is just enough room for him to sit on a stool. On the side is a newspaper. The horoscopes page is laid open.

Mrs Thorne was awake at quarter to seven. It was necessary to decamp from the living room and settle into the kitchen. His duty was to reassemble the cushions, and fold the cocoon.

She is a large woman. There is nothing wrong with being large, but her belief system is offensive.

'So you don't like to try new things,' she says.

'I do, sometimes.'

'But you seem quite straight-laced.'

This is probably a fair comment. He doesn't want to be dull, though.

You know you must be talking to someone irritating when you would rather see Barry. It's unfortunate that Barry is sleeping.

Then Mrs Thorne says he ought to consult a spiritual adviser. You get the impression she won't be happy until she's allowed to press hot crystals onto his back, or set his nostrils on fire. As far as she's concerned, there must be some therapy – some alternative to logic – that will cure his gloom. He would be the ultimate patient.

'I'll make you an appointment,' she says.

'You don't have to do that.'

'It's fine.'

'No, seriously.'

Then he wonders whether she's as repulsed by him as he is by her. If she were a politician she would be required to justify her stupidity. As it stands, there is no price for her ignorance.

You wonder what Barry must think. Barry will be missing his dominatrix.

The clock on the wall says seven-thirty. He should go.

The objective is to see Muriel. There is no comparison between Muriel and Mrs Thorne. Muriel is intelligent, and calm, and doesn't wear pashminas. She is talented, as well. It would be embarrasing to compare the two of them.

Then he says to Mrs Thorne that he should go.

She follows him into the hall, which is a surprise.

'So you're going to see your wife?' she says, opening the door.

'Yes.'

'Is she spiritual?'

'No.'

'You should see a spiritual adviser,' she says. 'Both of you.'

'I'm not sure.'

'You see!' she exclaims, as if she has found some irrefutable evidence. 'Straight-laced.'

This time he doesn't say anything.

He pulls his bag over his shoulder.

Then he exits the apartment and walks down the stairwell as fast as he can.

*

The walk will do him good.

The first thing you notice about the town is the wind. A brazen, cold wind that kicks up litter and turns the streets into a mess.

If he walks for long enough, something will happen.

Fate will lead him towards Muriel. His own mind and body should not have to be active participants. Fate will do the job.

The idea is not just to find Muriel, but also to stand in her favourite places. The idea is to feel the essence of the town.

Where is everyone? He would like to shake the town awake.

You would expect to see more people outdoors, but what is there to do? The town is not urban enough to accommodate fun. It's not rural enough to make your own entertainment. There is nowhere to ride a bicycle. It can't even be said to have faded grandeur, this part of town. The most that can be said is that it exists.

Just before the roundabout is a bookmakers.

There is a small convenience store called Premier Broadgate, known to the locals as Nigel, after the owner.

There is a Chinese takeaway combined with a chip shop. It has a television monitor with the rolling news, which seems inappropriate somehow. It reminds you that the world is still turning.

There is a snooker club, which doesn't have a name.

There is a gap in demand somewhere, but none of these buildings seem to fill it.

The hope is that if he walks for long enough he will find something.

It's only when he approaches the town centre that he starts to wonder if anyone will recognise him. The threat is real, rather than something imagined. The worry is allowed to linger in his mind, because he does nothing to stop it.

The relief in coming here is that nobody makes an effort. If the council were to erect a suitable welcome sign for the town, it would be accompanied with the words, 'where nobody makes an effort'. You don't have to dress up. You don't have to do anything.

He is glad to walk down the high street in the clothes that feel most comfortable. No-one likes to go home and feel like they don't belong. You have to be who you are.

Opposite the traffic island is the famous clock tower. It's not as famous as it used to be. It used to know the time.

Some of the shop fronts have wooden boards where there should be windows.

There is a tattoo parlour. It has a cartoon-style flame painted over the brick.

A café has white painted letters on the window. It says:

Tea and toast - £1

There is a sports shop displaying a selection of baseball bats. In England, there is no correlation between the number of baseball bats sold and the popularity of baseball.

In the main square is a statue of Queen Victoria. The square could be made beautiful but no-one will make the effort.

On the next street – although it can't be seen from here – are the ruins of a factory. It wouldn't take much to give the town a second life. If you ask the residents, a new factory would do it.

The best way to see the town is to avoid the main roads.

He decides to turn down a side street so that he may walk along the cobbles. It's nice to walk on the cobbles. It reminds him of something that has been lost. The motorway should be cobbled too.

He walks in the direction of the sea. You can smell the sea, even from here.

In the next street is a brick council estate named after existentialist philosopher Simone de Beauvoir.

Under the iron bridge is a rail depot where the tracks converge. On the other side is a derelict pub.

In front of him are the steps to the beach.

He thought he had said goodbye to the sea, but here it is. He thought he had lost sight of it forever. Something brought him back.

The sea is what redeems the town. Were it not for the sea, it would be hard to imagine a more desolate place.

The attraction of the sea is that he can look out and do nothing. This is a great pleasure. There is no land that he can see on the horizon, but there must be something. It would be tempting to use this moment to reflect, but there is nothing to gain just by reflecting. It would be a mistake to stand here and say the pebbles mean something more than they do. The rocks and sand mean nothing, just as the sea is simply water - lots of water. He knows nothing of these things, beyond the fact that they exist, and he exists with them. Nature is beyond his comprehension, which of course makes it no less beautiful. And there is nothing more beautiful than the sea. Nothing, at least, that he tends to experience. Mountains might compare, but there are no mountains in this town.

On the seafront there is not much in the way of landmarks, unless you consider the once-great pier or the once-great ballroom.

Just ahead of him are some rocks and a concrete jetty. There is a lifeboat museum, which is a brick bungalow with corrugated iron shutters. Further along is the pier itself. It's the kind of pier that, before the 1950s at least, would have been a place worth visiting.

Should he continue looking at the sea? No, he should leave it alone. It hasn't done him any good. He has been staring at the sea for long enough.

*

The house is just a short walk from the sea.

As a neighbourhood, it offers very little. There is nothing much to recommend it. The people are nice, though. Through some of the windows you can see people watching television.

Among the households, there is a mixture of incomes. Of the adults who work, most have public sector jobs in things like nursing and social services. Their parents, if they're still alive, are retired shipbuilders, almost exclusively. There has been a sea change, somewhere down the line.

The road has been repaired just once in memory. It has a pothole waiting to be filled.

The house is situated in the middle of the terrace. Theirs is the only house to have been painted. He always wanted to recommend a paint job to the neighbours. This way, everyone could pretend they're living in a pastel coloured house next to an ocean.

There is a postman depositing mail into the letter box. It makes him wonder if his name will be on the envelopes. You would have to assume so.

He could have called Muriel, of course. For some reason, he wanted to make it more dramatic than that. She will open the door and give him a hug. She will be delighted that he made the effort.

The living room curtains are closed.

The key is in his pocket, but he ought to knock.

He should knock and explain himself. He should explain that he has come all this way and she ought to let him inside. It will be a shock for her. You wonder if she has prepared for the visit. She might appear in her dressing gown and slippers. Or, worst of all, she might have a visitor. A man might be sitting in the bath. What a thought.

The worst thing is that it makes perfect sense. She has ignored him for so long.

Already it feels like the decision to come here was a bad idea.

If he could look at himself in the mirror, he wouldn't know what to think.

Then he decides that he would rather Muriel didn't come to the door. Instead, he would like to get away.

He is alarmed by the scrape of something.

Without making a noise, he is able to peer through the letter box.

Looking closer, he can see the envelopes on the carpet.

Then of course, everything is clear when the dog emerges.

The dog catches sight of him and, much to his alarm, begins to bark.

Then it barks again. The bark is louder than you would expect of a small dog. It steadies its hind legs and then hurries towards the door, where it jumps.

The next sight is of Muriel coming down the stairs.

'It's alright,' she says.

The decision to turn around requires no thought. It's something his body demands without the permission of his mind.

It's inexplicable, really, that he should run. But that's what he finds himself doing.

Then he surprises himself with his ability to run fast.

He must continue to run. He doesn't want to see the dog; he doesn't want to see some bloke in the bath.

The route will be the same way he came. The iron bridge… the rail depot… the derelict pub. If he reaches the sea, he will have lost her.

There are more people on the streets now. It's as though everyone decided to come out when they heard he was going mad. If he looks like a weirdo, it can only be a good thing. It will stop them from coming near.

Then he runs for a mile or so, but it feels like much further. It might as well be the other side of the ocean.

Twenty

You would think this might constitute a crisis.

It was stupid to do what he did. It was a long run. Then he came back and knocked on the door, which Mrs Thorne, to her eternal credit, was kind enough to open. Then he felt tired. Then he woke the next morning and was saddened to discover that he's still on this bloody planet.

It would be inaccurate to say that Mrs Thorne is tending to him. She is standing there without much regard for his plight. Of course, it would be wrong to expect anything more. She can hardly be expected to hoist him from the floor, can she?

Even with his eyes closed, he can tell that she is moving around the apartment in an agitated sort of way. She is concerned, no doubt, that he is taking up room. The atmosphere is no longer conducive to the business of faith healing.

In the next room she is shouting something like, 'Get him out of here!'

If Mrs Thorne has any healing powers, she ought to use them now. She could do a good job on him. She could make everything better.

Barry walks into the living room, muttering something about losing his cufflinks.

Barry opens a drawer and seems to do it loud on purpose.

It was considerate of Barry and his wife to let him sleep another night. The experiment is to see how long he can lie here. The floor cushions aren't such a bad arrangement. He could lie here for longer, with or without their permission.

Then he looks at Barry and says, 'How was your day?'

'Fine,' Barry says, looking for the remote. 'What have you done?'

'I watched television with your wife.'

'But you hate television.'

'I slept through most of it.'

Barry is shaking his head. You get the impression that Barry will shake his head and sigh at everything. Even if he had good news, Barry would sigh.

Barry points the remote at the television and says, 'Have you spoken to Muriel?'

'I'm not ready.'

'You've had ages,' Barry says. 'When are you going to pull your finger out?'

Mrs Thorne walks into the room. 'It's getting ridiculous.'

They are beginning to sound mean.

All he can say is, 'I don't want to be a burden.'

'You're acting like one,' Barry says.

'Fine. I'll sleep on the pavement.'

'You have a house down the road.'

'I'm not ready yet. I thought I was ready but I'm not.'

'When are you going to be ready?'

'Soon.'

If it comes down to it, he would rather sleep on the streets than go home. This is what he explains.

'You'd rather sleep on the streets?'

'Yes.'

Barry looks at his wife, and between them, they seem to have no idea what to do. It seems likely that Barry will shrug and say, fine - sleep on the streets. Instead, Barry turns around and says, 'I'll see you in a bit.'

'Where are you going?'

'Out.'

*

Mrs Thorne, for the next part of the afternoon, is successful at ignoring him. She must reckon that if she stays silent, he will go away.

She has been watching television for two hours, which has allowed him a sufficient length of time to do nothing. She is watching television for no reason other than habit.

In one sense, she has become more tolerant towards him. She knows that if she begins shouting, he will ignore her. She might as well just wait for him to leave on his own accord.

In a strange way, he has sympathy for Mrs Thorne. Barry, the gorilla in a suit, must be a terrible husband. You feel that if she really wanted, she could find another gorilla.

It would be too much to say there is a bond developing between them. She is tired, which reduces her ability to moan.

His own energy has been limited by the fact of his idleness. He has imposed speed restrictions on himself. It has been easy to sleep, but much harder to do things.

On the television there is some mention of the war, which makes him feel exhausted. Both sides of the House of Commons have been debating the idea of authorising military force, and with a handful of exceptions, they seem to agree that yes, it would be a good idea.

Mrs Thorne switches the channel.

They agree upon a programme - some sort of quiz.

She knows none of the answers, but continues, with some persistence, to watch the show. Then he supposes that Mrs Thorne must live like this all the time. She will sit in front of the television, answering quiz show questions, and pretending there is nothing else to live for.

In the advert break she says, 'Why don't you call your wife?'

'I will.'

'Here's the phone,' she says, passing the handset.

This is a trick.

He looks at the phone and says, 'I'll do it later.'

There is nothing to worry about. Nothing is wrong, really.

Muriel is doing alright. She has a dog, sure, but the only signs of a replacement husband are probably from his imagination. She might have a new man, or he might be imagining things. There are no signs that point towards anything.

Mrs Thorne is looking at him as if he's the mad one.

'You're a strange man,' she says.

They agree upon something.

Then he finds a comfortable position in the cocoon and lets his eyes close.

*

When he wakes for the next time, he wonders if he will ever wake in the apartment again. No-one is around, which makes it difficult to comprehend what might happen next. Have they left him alone? They might have finally decided it would be better to leave him alone. He can rest.

The longer the apartment is empty, the more he will feel alone. This is natural. It would be strange to feel anything else.

There is no objective. It has all become muddled. There is nothing left to do, which means there is nothing left to feel. You can only walk round the apartment so many times. His body is here, but the will is gone. You can't do anything without the will.

The inside of the apartment has begun to feel like the inside of his head. Outside of these walls, he conceives of nothing. It worries him to even think about the streets outside the building.

Then he worries about how bad he must look. To an outsider, he will look awful. He resembles something like a sick hospital patient in smart clothes. The flannel shirt has served him well. He dresses like a handsome man ought to, without being handsome.

He has the courage to step into the kitchen. There is no-one to stop him making some food. It no longer feels audacious to make himself a plate of toast. It feels like something owed to him. There is no reason to apologise for toast.

Should he enjoy his time alone? There is nothing to complain about. In actual fact, he ought to thank Barry and his wife when they return. They have allowed him to sleep, which is something to be grateful for. They have done more than might be expected. He has been able to live like a pig and get away with it.

How do you explain their generosity? Barry has never seemed like a generous person. It might be some kind of fear, or guilt. Or perhaps Barry might believe – wrongly – that he will get a decent meal in return.

The way in which he begins to make amends is to wash the dishes. In making himself useful, the hope is that he can stay a while longer. He could help with some of the ironing, but it would seem like a strange thing to do.

The radio is what annoys him. In his wet rubber gloves, he is forced to listen to the news bulletin. The only practical thing is to run the tap so he can block out the sound.

For some reason, the sound of running water makes him feel calm. It has a relaxing quality. It allows him to forget about everything.

He positions the final plate on the draining board.

Then he walks to the living room, where anything could happen.

The cushions are laid on the floor. Barry was right about the comfort. What Barry could never have anticipated was the occupation of his living room. It has been a long battle, but he is winning. He is winning at something.

If he could secure their permission, he would rent their apartment, but only six square feet in the lounge. It would leave them with plenty of room.

There is enough space to lie down.

He is satisfied there is nothing left to do. It's impossible to know what will happen next.

*

Somehow, he had managed to fall asleep again.

It's hard to imagine that he will be allowed to lie here much longer.

It must be night-time.

He wants to keep his eyes closed. The basis for keeping his eyes closed is the understanding that darkness is better than lamplight. If he could cover his ears, it would be ideal. Then he decides it would be impossible to keep his eyes closed forever.

He opens his eyes and is too confused to understand that Muriel is standing in front of him. She is standing there, for real, and not just in his imagination.

The sight of Muriel is too significant a thing to register all at once. It must be acknowledged for its significance and absurdity. No amount of rehearsal can prepare you for this. However many nights he spent awake, thinking about this moment, it was never likely to prepare him for it. It's the suddenness, and absurdity, that they should meet at this moment, that is difficult to accept. Why couldn't they meet earlier? For it to happen now is something to lament. To see Muriel in a grey knitted jumper is a disappointment. This is the piece of clothing she finds most relaxing.

She is looking at the trinkets in the wooden cabinet, as if she too cannot believe Barry owns anything of the sort.

It only feels like an actual human experience when she says, 'Joe.' There is no strength in his voice, so she continues, 'I'm coming home with you.'

'With me?'

'Is that alright?'

The Final Part

Twenty-One

They had forgotten about Daryl. This is what causes Daryl to open the fridge, and wonder what he might eat.

'I'm so sorry,' Rosalind says. 'I thought there would be enough.'

'It's alright,' Daryl says, removing some butter that he plans on spreading onto some bread.

If Daryl were honest about it, he would say that he's delighted to have dodged a bullet. The bowl of dhal doesn't look like his sort of thing. The shame, if anything, is more the fact they had forgotten about him. It's strange, as well, how much Rosalind wants to apologise, as if nothing could ever repair the damage.

'I'll make you something tomorrow,' she says.

'Don't worry, Rosalind.'

Daryl spends the next few seconds with his hand on the bread loaf. It would be unfair to take too much.

He begins to cut a slice.

The bread is better than the dhal.

At the table are a couple of lads who will probably dislike him.

Daryl pulls out a chair and decides, through guilt more than anything, that he should sit and watch them eat. It seems like a normal thing to do.

Now that he can look at them, there is something to consider. Is it possible to be cool and friendly? In the case of these guys, some people would consider them cool, but not many would consider them friendly. He would like to think they're neither.

One of them is sending a text message on his phone; the other lad is thumbing the buttons of a camera, smiling at something on the screen.

How long will he sit here before they say something? You might assume they're in a bad mood. But actually, it's nothing to do with a bad mood. They lack class.

George is sitting at the table, just opposite Rosalind. George is wearing a denim jacket, which makes him look older. George also has some stubble on his chin. George is someone who might challenge the theory. You could say that George is cool and kind.

Rosalind is nice, as well. She often talks about what he is going to do with his life. She asks him questions. For all her good intentions, though, she still thinks of him like a specimen in a zoo. She pretends that everything he says is fascinating, just because it comes from the mouth of someone who once slept under a bridge. Still, it's better to have your heart in the right place than to have no heart at all.

It would be hard to say who is hurting the most - George or Rosalind. One of them must love the other slightly more. They only seem to kiss when they're drunk, which is a good sort of deal, really.

'This is Daryl,' George says, for the benefit of the lads.

'Oh, cool,' someone says.

'Daryl does a bit of everything.'

There follows a list of things that Daryl might do in a typical day.

He might clean the bathtub. He might cook a meal. He might bleed the radiators.

In truth, he does a number of simple things that anyone could do. He is deserving of a basic level of respect, but not the incessant affection they smother him with. It makes Daryl wonder why they surround him with so much love. It makes him wonder what exactly they feel guilty about. But then again, the heart is there, so they can be forgiven.

George mentions how Bevan Breakfast has helped people like Daryl.

You would think George might follow this up with some other comment. Instead, George unscrews the wine bottle and pours another glass.

On the table is a small booklet that Rosalind had printed. It contains some of the details about the next exhibition, which focuses on the work of Muriel Street.

'It should be great,' George says, which is a comment designed to unite the room.

In fact, the rest of them agree that the exhibition will be amazing.

'I think Mum's looking forward to it,' Rosalind says.

George leans forward and says, 'Do you think they'll be alright?'

'Who?'

'Your mum and dad.'

'They'll be fine.'

On the table are some postcards labelled with the name Muriel. The postcards depict barren crop fields and scorched earth.

One of the lads is looking through the postcards and says, 'Nice.'

The other is nodding. And he too, says, 'Oh, nice.'

The lads have probably never heard of Muriel. Their fondness for the work is born of necessity. It would be remiss to say they dislike the postcards. This is probably what makes them lie. Imagine if they looked at the postcards and said they're all shit. It wouldn't happen.

'I like this one,' says the lad with the postcard.

'Yeah,' the other one says. 'There's a real starkness to it.'

It almost feels like there is a competition to decide who likes it the best.

'It's very monochrome,' one of them says. 'Is that the word?'

'Yeah.'

Sometimes Daryl feels like staying silent, and this is why. He would like to think there is a reason for his silence.

He is unable to think of any circumstance in which he could get along with these people. He wonders whether there is any need to make an effort. This is probably what makes him so quiet. It's doubtful that anyone would understand his desire to watch Match of the Day.

Rosalind is watching him. 'How are you, Daryl?' she says.

The question is not what he wanted to hear. There is an expectation that he will speak like a normal person. The expectation will be difficult to meet.

'Not so bad.'

'What have you been up to?'

'Well... '

He always knew that when the opportunity presented itself, like now, he should tell them the truth. He should say thank you, and good luck. He should say what a pleasure it has been to work among them. He should give them sufficient notice for the start of his new job. He should say how excited he is! He should say all these things, but when Rosalind looks at him and smiles, he actually says nothing.

It has been a good thing, coming here. It's not an evil house, or anything. The people who thought of Bevan Breakfast should take much of the credit. It has been a good experience, but not so good that he might want to work here forever. There is nothing stable about the way in which he lives. He would like an address. Whilst he is grateful for the work, and the occasional night on the sofa, it was always going to be something temporary.

Unless he speaks, the conversation will die.

So Daryl looks at Rosalind and says, 'I've been offered a job.'

This is something he should have said a couple of hours ago. He was thinking about what to say, but couldn't get the words out.

'That's brilliant,' Rosalind says. 'I'm really happy for you.'

George reaches out and says, 'Nice one, buddy.'

Even the lads are smiling. This is what they hoped a freewheeling guesthouse would look like.

Then Rosalind says things like, 'oh, well done,' as if she had just heard the news this split second.

When you think about it, they will be delighted. They might congratulate themselves. They might see it as their triumph. It's hard to avoid the symbolism. Here is Daryl - the first success story of Bevan Breakfast. They might arrange a mosaic of his face.

Twenty-Two

Muriel is silent. You would think that having spent the last two months apart from her husband that she might have something to say.

She is sitting in the backseat, which means he is unable to look at her without turning around. There is a newspaper folded open on her lap. She has been reading something from the arts section.

He wants to say, what are you so quiet for?

If he weren't such a coward, he could ask the question. In the absence of courage, silence dominates. He should have known the journey would be like this. He shouldn't have expected anything else. Muriel has placed a high price on her forgiveness.

It's a good thing they decided to drive home at night. The tiredness gives them an excuse to be silent.

The backseat has been encumbered with picture frames and boxes. It makes the car feel smaller. There is a canvas just over his shoulder, protruding from behind. If it weren't for the boxes, he would be sitting in the backseat too. Muriel could rest against his shoulder.

The weird thing is that no-one had told him about the exhibition. It was never billed as an event he ought to attend. It must have been scheduled in his absence.

Barry is sitting with his hands on the wheel, and has taken it upon himself to remain silent. The theory is that silence is more congenial for the husband and wife. Silence will allow them to overcome their differences.

Barry winces and lets out a yawn. This is probably a cue for something.

'Does anyone want to play a game?'

There is silence, which most people would take as a rejection.

Barry looks aside and says, 'How about you, Muriel?'

'Not right this minute.'

'Are you alright?'

'I'm fine. I'm just going to close my eyes.'

'Do you want me to wind down my window?'

'No, it's alright.'

It doesn't matter to Barry that Muriel might feel ill. Barry is unconcerned about the human aspect. The danger for Barry is that Muriel will vomit in his car. This is what worries Barry.

'We'll stop in a minute.'

*

The service station resembles an air traffic control tower. It has an enclosed bridge, some petrol pumps, and a large discount hotel. It must have been conceived as some kind of joke. It's a pit stop for humans.

You can never step inside a service station without feeling some kind of regret. Where else would such a large number of people walk into a building that, in an ideal world, none of them would visit?

The concourse has a general store, some arcades and a wall of payphones. Everyone looks tired. No-one wants to hang around for long. The parents, especially, want to load the car and go.

There is a restaurant that, under any circumstances, would be a terrible place to eat.

Then he gestures with his hand that Muriel should find a table.

At the counter he orders a coffee and some water.

The coffee comes with a napkin, which seems unnecessary.

Barry, perhaps in order to let them talk alone, announces that he's going to the toilet.

There is a table at the back, with its own collection of dirty plates. You suspect that no-one will come and clean the table.

Muriel is sitting on the plastic swivel chair.

She is wearing a denim coat. She is going to keep her arms crossed, just so she feels protected. Her hair is still grey, which is a relief. The worry was that she might have had a breakdown. She might have dyed her hair black.

She is looking beyond the floor-to-ceiling glass. There is nothing to look at.

She allows herself to look at him. 'What are you thinking about?' she says.

'You.'

This is probably too much.

He stirs the coffee with a plastic stirrer and says, 'How've you been?'

'Terrible.'

'What's wrong?'

He puts a hand on her shoulder, which carries no risk, given what she said. She does nothing to deflect the hand away. Nor is she smiling. She wants to say something. What does she want to say? She will probably tell him something terrible.

'I'm sorry that I haven't spoken to you.'

'That's okay.'

'I don't have an excuse,' she says.

'You don't need one.'

'I'm just sorry.'

She has run out of times she can say sorry. She has said it enough.

She looks through the glass and watches the forecourt, which looks like an airport runway. You can almost imagine a plane coming in to land.

He begins to understand that her distractedness is all a

front. She is distracted by nothing; she is focused on some terrible thought. She is avoiding whatever is making her sad.

She is gripping the cup of coffee. She doesn't want to let it go. She doesn't want to break down. All the emotion is going to make her cry. You can just tell.

There is no reason to remove his hand from her shoulder. The hand is resting there when he says, 'Why don't we just go back to how we were?'

She puts the scrunched napkin to her nose. 'I just want to get through this weekend.'

'And then what?'

'Then we'll see.'

She could have said something more. She could have said what she was thinking, at least.

Then, probably for the sake of convenience more than anything, she says, 'I feel a bit sick.'

The only way to respond is to lean closer.

Then he allows himself to reach his arm across her shoulder. This is what the moment demands. This is about as tender as you can be without feeling self-conscious in a service station.

He feels more like a husband than he did just a moment ago.

It would be nice if they could forget about everything. He would like to take her home - wherever that might be. It would be nice if they could start again.

*

In the car, there is no question as to whether he will sit next to Muriel. The answer is no.

Rather than think about what she said – which was something about getting through the weekend – he ought to close his eyes and forget about everything. He could forget he ever came on the journey. Someone will wake him.

The radio is playing music, but no-one has been concentrating enough to care about it. The radio can do what it likes.

His feet are resting in their preferred position; in fact, he is comfortable in a physical sense. The emotional part is more difficult. If he were more confident about the situation, he would reach out a hand so that Muriel might clench it. He couldn't be sure that she would clench it, though.

Her arms are folded; her eyes are closed. She has shut herself down.

She said she needed to get through the weekend. What exactly does this mean? It's hard to understand. She's on a different frequency.

She is definitely asleep; she doesn't have the will for consciousness. If she wanted to talk, she would have stayed awake. But she doesn't, and she didn't.

Barry is looking at the road.

It's a credit to Barry, and a surprise, that such a volatile person could drive in such a dependable way. Barry has become someone he can rely on. You have to give the man credit, albeit not too much. He wouldn't want to give Barry any sort of victory.

The impression is that Barry wants to say something. Barry has been looking across – intermittently – for a good while.

'It's alright,' Barry says.

'What's alright?'

'I'm just saying. It's alright.'

It might be a general statement. Everything is alright. Barry might be referring to everything.

The circumstances, which include the presence of Muriel, make him grateful for Barry. It would be more awkward without Barry, which is something he never thought would be the case. He feared that Barry would irritate him the whole way home. He never thought that Barry would remain silent for so long. He never thought that Barry would become almost like a friend. Things must be bad, then.

'You can put what you want on,' Barry says, in reference to the radio.

'It's alright. I'm happy with silence.'

*

The walk between the car and the front door is carried out, like most of the journey, in silence.

The Bevan Breakfast sign makes the house look more inviting. It softens the effect of the iron gates.

There is no music from inside, if you can tell as much from standing at the front door. This is probably owing to some kind of respect for Muriel.

It doesn't feel like a homecoming. You almost expect people to jump out and yell surprise.

It's only when he opens the front door and drops his bag in the hall that he says, 'She must be asleep.'

This is good news. He wouldn't want to talk to Rosalind just now. It requires more thinking time.

The hall is silent. If it weren't for the lamplight, everything would be dark.

This is the moment he had wondered about. Where is he supposed to sleep?

Muriel, due to tiredness, and whatever else, begins to climb the staircase and says, 'Goodnight.'

'Where are you sleeping?'

'In the attic.'

You get the impression she hadn't thought about the sleeping plans. It hadn't struck her as something significant.

In an ideal situation, he would sleep in the attic. It's not like the attic belongs to him, but it would be reasonable to assume he might sleep there. He might as well ask.

'Where should I sleep?'

'I don't know.'

It would make sense to bring Barry into it. This would reduce the extent of his embarrassment.

'What about Barry?'

She is standing with her hands in her coat pockets. She is protected this way.

Then she frowns and says, 'Why don't you both sleep on

the couch?'

This is probably what she always assumed they would do.

In a way, he knew what to expect. She was never going to invite him upstairs.

What about tomorrow night? What about all the other nights?

Imagine a situation where Muriel never leaves.

He will become a resident of the couch. He will complement the other furnishings. He will sleep in the eye of the storm. This is what will happen. He had better get used to it.

*

He flicks the light. The room is lit and someone murmurs.

Daryl is there, spread across the couch. The little woodland creature is under a blanket. He had forgotten about Daryl. What he hadn't anticipated – but what he should have remembered – is that Daryl sometimes sleeps in the living room.

Daryl has just enough energy to rouse himself and say, 'Eh?'

'It's alright, Daryl.'

Daryl is satisfied enough to close his eyes.

The couch is something Daryl has become accustomed to. In all likelihood, it's something that he, too, will learn to love or hate.

Barry, in a white string vest, enters the living room. Upon noting Daryl's presence, Barry says, 'Do you want me to wake him?'

'Why would you do that?'

It would seem reasonable to leave Daryl alone.

Barry is smiling as if there were something soft about letting Daryl sleep. 'As you wish,' Barry says.

Barry lowers himself into the armchair, with a blanket wrapped around his belly. Without making it official, Barry has reserved the armchair. In the world of Barry, there is no such thing as diplomacy.

It feels like there is nowhere else to go.

Muriel has decreed that the attic is out of bounds.

What is the contingency plan? The question remains as to where he might sleep.

If he were to move the coffee table, there would be enough space.

He stands in front of the table and, without the help of Barry, pulls it aside.

He manages to create a space next to the extension lead.

Then, with the cushions from the furniture, he makes a bed for himself. Were it not for the cushions, things would be problematic.

Then he lays down the cocoon, which will enable him to sleep.

Everything is done.

He is able to lower himself under the duvet.

What comes next is the obvious thing.

The silence, which accompanies the darkness, makes him want to talk.

Is there any point in trying to sleep? He will be awake all night, alone with his thoughts, which is all he ever seems to be.

It might be a good idea if he says something aloud. If he speaks, it would make amends for the sleeplessness.

So he imagines that Barry is listening and says, 'Thanks for everything.'

You can tell that Barry is almost asleep, which is something to be jealous about. It takes a few seconds for Barry to say, 'Thanks for what?'

It's important to maintain a passive voice. No emotion. A certain amount of discipline is required.

'For driving us down.'

'It's fine,' Barry says. 'No dramas, mate.'

What comes next is the silence, which has the potential to last. He would like to break the silence.

'Do you think it's good enough just to be a nice person?'

Barry is listening, without having the strength to make a sentence.

Then, due to obligation more than anything, Barry says, 'What kind of question is that?'

'I've been thinking.'

'About what?'

'Whether it's good enough just to be nice.'

'Sure it is.'

'Is it enough, though?'

'What else are you supposed to be?'

'Committed to something.'

This time, the silence has some kind of purpose. Barry is thinking.

'I think you're committed,' Barry says. 'What about this place?'

'What about it?'

Barry points at the couch and says, 'The fact that lad can sleep here instead of the gutter is all because of you.'

There is more feeling in the words this time. Barry is winning the fight against sleep.

'That's all you need to remember,' Barry says.

There is reason to believe that Barry is talking sense. You would hope so. It would be nice to have confirmation of his worth.

What next? A normal person would close their eyes and sleep. You get the impression it will be more difficult than that.

Sleep is what he wants.

The darkness is not such a bad thing. Nor is the silence.

The only thing he can resent Barry for is the great snore, which begins shortly afterwards, and continues for most of the night.

Twenty-Three

The exhibition is called Muriel Street - Damaged Landscapes. The photographs depict – for the most part – a series of ravaged fields from which flowers, against the odds, have managed to grow. The most popular one is called 'Empty Field, Weston-super-Mare'. There are portraits, too. In the hall is a portrait of what looks like a business owner – a car salesman, or something – who is sitting with his feet on the desk. You could look at the picture all day and it still wouldn't make much sense. It doesn't matter, though. As long as it makes sense to Muriel, it's alright. That's the important thing.

There are more people in attendance than he had expected. They are looking at the photographs in silence. What is everyone thinking? It would be a good idea to familiarise himself with the general view, which is probably that the work is excellent. Most of them will wait for someone to give an opinion before they give their own. This is how it will go.

Just to the right is a woman in a pink cotton blouse who, without being aware of it, has trod on his foot. She is looking at a photograph of an allotment.

'I love this,' she says.

'It's extraordinary,' says a tall, silver-haired man with glasses. 'Look at the colours.'

'I know.'

There is a queue of people crowding into the studio, which encourages him to follow, and peer his head so that he might get a closer look.

Muriel, though taken with shawls on some days, is wearing a formal black dress. She is dressed like she has been waiting for the occasion. The exhibition must have been in her thoughts for a while.

She is standing in front of a picture frame, which she indicates with her hand. The image is a barren field with a scarecrow. She explains the meaning behind it, which draws upon her experience of isolation.

'I was in a bad mood,' she says.

Then she explains, in carefully chosen words, how she went about creating the piece. She mentions how the film was rinsed in acid at a specific room temperature. It would appear that she still has complete faith in her own talent.

Barry, who had an urgent meeting to attend, would have laughed about everything. Barry is the sort of person who would dismiss photography, and relegate it to some kind of hobby status. Barry would say the whole thing is a joke. There would be nothing to reflect upon. It's a bunch of pictures - live with it. That's what Barry would have said.

*

In the passage of time between listening to Muriel and wandering alone in the hall, what surprises him is how simple the photographs are. There is nothing that should make him feel intimidated. It was probably stupid of him to expect otherwise.

There is no particular thought in his mind when he climbs the staircase. There are less people on the landing than the living room. It means he can move without inhibition and without caring about whether he looks normal enough.

Beyond the second floor there are no more guests. No-one has discovered the third floor. Then he reaches the top landing. The light is coming from the bedroom.

He is conscious that he has roughly two seconds to make a decision. It would appear his legs have already decided. And when he twists the door handle, and peers inside, the sight of Muriel is what he expected.

She is looking at the mirror. She is removing some earrings, conscious of his presence and happy to allow it. If she were worried, she would have turned around.

She is unable to smile, though. The least you might expect is a smile. It's almost as if she has become resigned to her fate - whatever that might be.

She seems to have been working on something. An old camera is positioned on the table. Some photographs are laid there.

When he sits on the bed, there is nothing to suggest that she might join him too. In fact, she remains in front of the mirror.

It does him no good to see her so calm. He would like her to be tense, or at least she could pretend to be. What is there to be calm about? Is she so confident their marriage is over that she doesn't need to give an explanation? It's a shame he must rely on guesswork. You couldn't say she seems happy, but neither does she seem hostile. If anything, she is unaffected.

She sighs, which makes him suspicious. Why would she sigh unless she has something bad to say? She is readying him for the pain. In a non-violent way, she is sticking a knife into him.

The difficulty is about whether he should talk first. Should he pre-empt the disaster? There is so much to say, but he should start with the thing that hurts the most.

'Are you seeing someone?'

The only thing to do, and the only thing that matters at all, is to discover the truth.

She is unable to look at him.

She looks at the floor, which is the best, most eloquent way of answering the question.

'I'm sorry,' she says.

He lacks the passion to scream aloud. He would like to scream, but it would be weird. A scream would not be worthy of his temperament.

Now he can say that he is lost. There is no way in which he can reclaim any dignity. It has gone.

There are questions, but he doesn't know how to ask them.

Is it necessary for him to show some emotion? No. He is beyond emotion. He is post-emotion.

'He's a musician,' she says.

She is looking at the mirror.

Then, after the silence, she continues, 'He's touring at the moment.'

'What kind of music?'

'Folk.'

This is a shame. It would be nice if there were an obvious weakness. It's a shame that Muriel likes folk music.

If you take sentiment out of it, the most sensible thing would be to leave. But sentiment is never out of it.

It would be ideal if you could tell – by the look on her face – that she regrets everything. A quiver would do, but it won't happen. She regrets nothing. She is calm; she is certain of the words that leave her mouth. And he, by contrast, is certain of nothing.

'I was probably hoping you would find someone,' she says.

She retrieves a camera and looks through the viewfinder. She puts the camera down.

'Have you not enjoyed your freedom?'

'No.'

'Have you met anyone?'

'No-one.'

She is looking for something on the desk and says, 'I thought you'd have met someone.'

'Well, I haven't.'

She lifts one of the cardboard trays. She positions the tray on the bed.

'I've done so much these past few weeks. I must have taken a thousand pictures.'

'I've done nothing.'

She is looking at the tray, and deciding whether to straighten the contents.

'But you've done so much good,' she says. 'Look at this place.'

'I did it for you.'

'No you didn't,' she says. 'It's a wonderful achievement. And you should be proud.'

The worst thing is that he's unable to hate Muriel. It's impossible, because she doesn't invite hatred by the way she is.

She removes a biro from the tray. She runs the tip against a page. There is no ink.

'You've inspired me,' she says. 'I feel like there's so much I want to do.'

'Why can't you do it with me?'

She ignores this.

'There's something tangible about what you've done.' She is waiting for a response. After the silence, she says, 'Don't you feel it?'

'I don't know what I feel.'

'You've made something real,' she says. 'You've made a system.'

She is looking at him, almost as if she wants to impress upon him some important point. By the way she speaks, you would think there is something to celebrate.

The black dress has the effect of making her look thinner. If she asked for his opinion he would discourage her from wearing the black dress. She is thin enough already. Granted, the folk musician may see something different.

She is beginning to realise that he has no desire to speak.

She puts a hand on his palm and says, 'It's not something I planned.'

'It's alright.'

'I just think we're not the same people anymore.'

'I suppose.'

'I think we became the worst version of ourselves.'

She is waiting for him to speak. There is nothing to say.

So she says, 'I thought you'd have realised this.'

There is probably some logic in what she says. Even if the words made no sense, it wouldn't matter. Everything has been decided. There is not enough time.

If he had planned it better, he would have told her he loves her. He would have made an emotional pitch. She would need some convincing, of course, but it would have been worth it.

Why is he still in the room? There have been opportunities to leave, but something has convinced him to stay. It's the idea that he might rouse himself at any moment. It's the idea that he has nothing to lose, so he might as well stay.

'I haven't asked you about the exhibition,' she says. 'What do you think of it?'

'I like it.'

'I know you think it's all rubbish.'

It takes a moment to decide his response. She is probably right.

'That's not fair.'

'I'm right, though.'

'I liked the car salesman.'

'Why?'

'I don't know.'

'Did you like the colours?'

'Not just that.'

She is intelligent enough to know when he's lying.

It's true that he liked the photographs. She will accept this. What she will reject is the notion that it made an emotional connection. His emotional involvement was zero.

'You know you're good.'

'It's not about being good,' she says. 'I could be the best in the world and no-one would notice.'

It seems odd that she needs to dismiss her own worth. He will never understand it.

He ought to go, really. There is an exhibition to endure. He should discover a picture that he likes and store it in his mind for conversational purposes.

The future is something to discuss another day.

The assumption is that he will regain control of the attic. Everything that belongs to him has been put in a pile under the desk. He will need to unpack his things again. Muriel will be gone.

She reaches for his hand.

'I'm sorry, Joe.'

There is nothing to say.

She begins to walk alongside him, as if she's showing him to the door. It makes him feel like he has no business in the bedroom.

She looks at him, attempting to make eye contact.

'I understand how you must feel.'

'Do you?'

'Of course.'

The longer she stands in front of him, the more it becomes obvious what she's alluding to. She doesn't need to say it.

'You know our history as well as I do.'

'But it's history.'

'Then we should probably stop talking about it.'

*

If he could decide these things, he wouldn't bother going downstairs. There would be some kind of panic room where he could punch a wall. There would be something to destroy. In the absence of something, his only hope is to smile. If you smile, you can disguise anything.

The dilemma is about what to do next. There is a certain level of commitment he ought to show. It would be unfair to disappoint Rosalind. Everything else is unimportant.

The only way of relaxing is to stand on the landing. He leans over the banister and listens to the music. What is there to be afraid of? He should embrace everything. This is his party as well.

*

The oddest thing is to peer inside the living room, where a group of women are sitting. At the sight of his face, they say his name in a kind of unison. He allows himself to smile in their presence.

George is positioned on the armrest. In his tweed jacket and soft leather boots, George has reached the next stage in his development as a hipster. Next will come the beard - a proper one, at any rate.

This is supposed to be an art exhibition. You wouldn't notice just by looking at George, who is making the women laugh with his stories.

Rosalind is standing next to George. You could say she has been effortless in her choice of clothes – a dotted blouse – which is what makes her look cool, in a lazy definition of coolness.

When you look around, it's difficult to know what to do next. The concern is that he has no obvious way of getting through the night. It's hard to say where the reprieve might come from. There is nothing he can do – short of setting his hair on fire – to get anyone's attention.

There is a kind of open letter he'd like to send everyone. Please don't just stand there and wait for me to speak. Or, understand, at the very least, that if you're happy to stand in silence, then I'm happy too.

Rosalind is looking at him, which she has probably been doing the whole time.

Without wanting to draw anyone's attention, she leans forward and says, 'Are you alright?'

This is the only thing that could make him cry. The sight of his daughter with a hand on his shoulder is the one thing that could do it.

'I hope you're okay,' she says.

This is vague enough. She is probably referring to Muriel, and the exhibition. This is probably what she meant.

If he tells one lie, he should say that he's having a good time.

'I'm enjoying myself.'

'Are you, though?'

If he thinks about this for long enough, he can convince himself of anything. That's the beauty of losing your mind.

'I'm fine.'

If she were satisfied with this, she would smile. Instead, she looks down at the floor.

'I haven't said thank you,' she says.

Then he asks what she needs to say thank you for.

She is too embarrassed to look at him. 'You were nice about Keith.'

'What else would I have done?'

'Of course,' she says. 'But you looked after me. That's why I want to say thank you.'

You can tell she hasn't finished yet. She would usually get up and walk somewhere. She has something else to say.

She explains that he has made the house somewhere worth living.

'I know it must have been difficult coming here,' she says.

'I had no choice.'

'It took a lot of courage. I won't lie, Dad. I hated you for a while.'

The part about hating him almost escapes his attention. The remarkable thing is that she referred to him as Dad. This is a remarkable thing.

'Do you hate me now?'

'No.' She smiles in a way that suggests she is telling the truth. 'And you introduced me to George,' she says. 'I'm not sure what I'll do about him.'

'Do what you like.'

'I'll probably break his heart.'

'I'm sure it will mend.'

She makes an effort to stifle her laughter.

She will enjoy life, then. This is good enough.

Then Rosalind pulls him towards the group of women.

'This is my dad,' she says.

She lets them have a closer look.

It will be easy to introduce himself, but harder to sustain a conversation.

The first woman leans closer. He was supposed to kiss her cheek.

He is persuaded to lean towards the next. The problem is that she would rather do a handshake.

By the time he is introduced to the tallest, he doesn't know what to do.

The relief is that laughter breaks out. It's not a menacing laughter, but rather, the kind that involves him too. They will cause him no harm.

The women are friends with Rosalind, and you can imagine them attending the same art exhibitions. He has forgotten their names already.

There is a heavy fringed woman in a tunic. She leans towards him and says, 'I love what you've done here.'

'Thank you.'

All three of them are smiling as if they share the same opinion.

'You've done a wonderful job,' she says.

She mentions that she works for a charity. She has already spoken to Rosalind about the possibility of running art classes for children with disabilities.

Rosalind puts an arm around him and says, 'I thought we could use the studio.'

'Of course.'

Rosalind mentions how they might wish to expand the scope of the project. It could encompass, say, hospitality training for the long-term unemployed. They could provide a meeting place for the elderly. There is plenty that can be done, Rosalind says.

Somehow, the conversation descends into a discussion – prompted by the woman in the tunic – about how great he is.

Without having planned for this to happen, the conversation is about him, his unconquerable spirit, and his compassion for the homeless. They are all in agreement.

'It's an incredible story,' says the one with the biggest forehead.

The forehead remains in his thoughts until she says, 'You've done an amazing job,' at which point he is able to concentrate on her kindness.

'That's very kind.'

The third woman taps him on the sleeve and says, 'It's wonderful how you and Rosalind have such a connection.'

And he allows himself to smile. The smile is appropriate, because of what they are saying. It's true that he is proud of Rosalind.

The difference with these guests, compared with the ones he has met previously, is that they are capable of performing simple acts of kindness. They love art, and have a suspicion of the business world, but they can talk to you about anything.

It would be nice to spend a whole day listening to how magnificent his work has been. If he wanted to, it would be possible. It's not clear whether they have a loyalty to Muriel, or Bevan Breakfast. The most important thing is that he's welcome.

There are more people in the living room than you might think.

Daryl is serving champagne from a tray. Daryl shouldn't have to smile. The lad should do as he pleases. You would hope they behave nicely to Daryl. You would hope they show him some respect.

George senior, who is looking well, despite his seventy-odd years, manages to reach out a hand.

'Hello, friend,' George senior says. 'I hope you're enjoying yourself.'

'Indeed, George.'

'Let me say,' George senior begins, and you suspect he might finish with something complimentary. 'You've done a marvellous job.'

All he can say is thank you, and what a pleasure it has been to work alongside the younger George.

'He's a good kid,' George senior says.

They leave it at that.

If they wanted, they could remark upon the physical contact between Rosalind and George, the two of whom, without any self-consciousness, are now holding hands. It would seem natural, if a little awkward, to mention this subject. In an unspoken way, they decide between the two of them to make nothing of it.

George senior tightens the jumper, which, true to form, is tied around his waist.

'I want to give you something,' George senior says. 'I believe you can turn this place into something special.'

George senior reaches into his pocket, from which he removes a chequebook. Then George senior rests it on the table and begins, in a slow, uncertain way, to write something. George senior peers across at the television to see the date – 20th March. You can see the level of concentration when George senior writes; you can see the tip of his tongue, as if George senior were preparing his saliva for the purposes of turning a page.

George senior tears the cheque and, with a proud sort of glance, passes it across.

'That should keep you going.'

'This is very generous, George.'

'It's my pleasure.'

It doesn't take long for Rosalind and then George to notice that something significant has happened.

'How wonderful,' Rosalind says.

George has no hesitation in giving his father a hug.

Everyone is pleased about what has happened. There is nothing to say, except thank you.

'Hang on,' Rosalind says, gesturing for Daryl to come closer. 'I would like to make a toast.'

Daryl, alarmed at the sudden responsibility, begins to pour champagne into each of their glasses.

Rosalind raises her glass. She says she would like to propose a toast to George senior. She says that everyone at Bevan Breakfast is proud to be associated with the man. The donation will contribute towards community outreach programmes. Everything is looking good.

'So thank you for this incredible gesture, George.'

There is a cheer from the women on the couch. Some of the other guests are clapping.

Then, in recognition of etiquette, George senior reaches for a spoon and clinks the stem of his glass.

'Thank you, Rosalind.'

George senior proposes a toast to his son, as well as Rosalind, and of course, the indefatigable Joe Street.

This time, there are more people cheering. The applause is sustained for a longer period.

There seems to be a general agreement that Bevan Breakfast has been a triumph. There is enough certainty in the room for everyone to congratulate themselves. Well done, then. Everything has worked out fine.

There is another clink of glasses, which poses an instant question. Who else wants to make a toast? There is no-one else. George has left the room. Muriel has gone somewhere. Then, when the voice announces itself with a plea for silence, the person who makes himself visible is Daryl.

'Hello, everyone,' Daryl says, just about loud enough to remain audible. 'I just wanted to say that I've really enjoyed my time here.'

This brings an immediate round of applause.

Some of the guests look at each other, as if they had never expected Daryl was capable of speaking.

'In particular, I want to thank Joe,' the lad continues.

There is a more committed round of applause at the mention of his name. It seems that everyone is determined to clap.

'I know he doesn't smile much, but I think he has a good heart.'

The noise from the audience is something like laughter. Some of them smile; some of them are keen to show how sweet they think Daryl is.

'This place has pulled me back from the brink, really. I don't know what I would have done without it.'

The way in which Daryl is holding the bottle of champagne suggests he daren't spill any of it. You can bet that everyone feels guilty that Daryl has to serve champagne.

Many of the people who occupied the studio have begun entering the living room. They want to see what the applause is all about. They want an explanation as to why they might need to clap. The reason is Daryl. The lad, who has never spoken at such length, is becoming a hero.

'Thanks to Bevan Breakfast, I'm happy to say that I've just found a new job,' Daryl says.

The applause, this time, has a more genuine feel, without the guilt that motivated the earlier round.

Daryl mentions that he will be working as a turnstile operator for Leyton Orient, his football club, and religion. You can tell this means nothing to ninety percent of the audience. It means something to Daryl, though.

'But today is about Joe. He started this project in the first place and he deserves all our support. I hope you will join me in raising your glasses.'

Everyone is doing it. All of them are doing what Daryl said. Daryl is the conductor. Then, predictably, there is a cheer.

The only thing to do is walk to the front.

He places a hand on Daryl's shoulder, almost as if he were addressing a child of his own.

'Thank you, Daryl.'

He hadn't expected they would hug, but this is what happens. They hug well.

'I'll remember you guys,' Daryl says.

'We'll remember you.'

There was nothing to ever suggest he might have inspired Daryl. Even now, it's difficult to understand what's happening.

Rosalind steps forward to address the room.

'Thanks so much everyone,' she says. 'There is plenty more to come. Daryl will be serving some chilli. So if you like burritos and beautiful photography, you've come to the right house!'

By the sound of the cheer, you can already guess their views on chilli.

The photographs will continue to inspire.

Everyone will eat something, and there will be nothing wrong in the world.

*

Nothing much happens until he finds himself at the salad bar. This is where most of the conversations are happening. What brought him to this side of the room was the impossibility of seeing Muriel. She is somewhere on the other side.

There is no reason to leave. Nothing that Muriel said should result in him leaving. There is an exhibition to finish. There is no use wondering how long it will go on for. It will go on all night.

Someone says his name. It's not a good enough reason to look up from the lettuce.

The voice sounds more familiar when she says, 'Do you remember me?'

He should probably turn around. He should try to understand what he ought to remember.

At the sight of this woman, who has big earrings and thick brown hair, he is reminded of Hammersmith, his drunkenness, and how cold it was that night. He can remember, as well, that her name is Lauren.

She had spoken to him with fantastic passion. She had made him think about doing something of value. She had stressed upon him the importance of helping others. And she was right, wasn't she? She was right to say he needed some sort of conviction.

'We met in the pub,' she says. 'I told you about my dissertation.'

'I remember.'

Just the thought of that night makes him feel tight in his stomach. The night went well, in some senses. Otherwise it was a disaster.

'I'm sorry if I barracked you at the time.'

'It's alright. It was deserved.'

'It's unbelievable what you're doing.'

In the way she looks at him, she really does believe that it's unbelievable. She is smiling in a way that makes her seem in awe of him. She doesn't want to admit it, but awe is the word. It makes him wonder what everyone is so excited about. Yes, you could say that Daryl is making a better life. There will be other Daryls, too. But until then, it doesn't feel like everything is perfect. They have contributed more to the world of art than social justice.

Lauren is looking at him as close as she can. She must be wondering if there's some secret he's not letting on. There must be a reason why he's not smiling.

'Do you remember when I told you to make yourself useful?'

'Yes.'

'Well, you've done it.'

'I suppose.'

'You've reinvented yourself.'

He would rather she said *redeemed*, but reinvented is fine.

Muriel is somewhere else, talking about cameras. Muriel is moving on.

'What have you planned next?'

'Oh, nothing much.'

'What about politics?'

'This is politics. I've never felt so political.'

He has never felt so alone, either. This isn't something he

wants to say.

Then Lauren says how she could easily write a new paragraph – a whole new chapter, in fact – were she to write her dissertation again.

'I love the fact you're helping people,' she says. 'That's what a politician is supposed to do.'

'But I'm not a politician.'

'Well, exactly.'

She is looking at him without emotion. She is waiting to discover what the catch might be.

'You're very modest,' she says.

Despite her intelligence, she has made the mistake of assuming he is proud of himself. He is proud of Rosalind, who has shown fantastic courage. Daryl is also a good lad. And for the most part, he can excuse George for his love of cardigans. He is proud of everyone, but not so much himself.

Then it becomes clear that Lauren is no longer keen to talk. She is looking away from him.

It's nice that she came alone, without her friends, which shows some kind of commitment. If she thought it was just an excuse to have fun, she would have brought her friends.

She is still distracted by something when she says, 'It's terrible, isn't it?'

By the way she looks at him, it's obvious that he ought to know what she's talking about. The trouble is that he has no idea.

Something happens that makes Lauren walk ahead.

It only takes a few seconds, but most of the guests are now standing in front of the television.

On the screen you can see a night sky and what looks almost like a fireworks display. The guests are no longer speaking about photography. Something more important has emerged.

There is a reporter with a camera crew, standing on a balcony. The grey-haired reporter looks into the lens.

'There are more air raids to come before British and

American ground forces make their move.'

The war has begun. He couldn't tell you which side is going to win. There will be a cabinet meeting happening right now, but what does he know about it? Ignorance is a luxury, and he is grateful to possess it. It's better to be ignorant than to focus on death.

It's more interesting to listen to the guests than the television. The consensus, which seems like a reasonable view, is that the war will be a disaster. It will bring death upon humans who aren't scheduled to die. And the more he starts to think about it, the more it feels shameful that he hasn't been following the news. What has he been doing? It might have been better if he had spent his whole time stopping the war. It's true that what's happening on the screen is something brutal, and wrong. It almost makes him want to apologise to the room.

Lauren is looking at the screen. It seems right that they should share this moment together. She was right when she said it was terrible. What's almost as bad is the fact he has done nothing at all – in a formal sense – to express his disgust. It's terrible.

'At least, with what you're doing, you're like a force for healing in the world,' she says.

Does she really mean this?

She wants him to insist that yes, there are some things worth believing in. Not everything is rotten in the world. The will to love is greater than the will to destroy.

You could say anything during this moment and it would seem profound. Anything will go down in history.

'I suppose this is one of those moments we'll always remember.'

These are the words he decides upon. Then he continues, 'Something good will eventually come of this. People will reject the next war.'

'Do you think so?'

Without answering, he is encouraged to develop his

thought, and surprises himself by suggesting there are two essential life forces at work - creation and destruction.

'If you have a wound, it will eventually heal.'

This is probably all he wanted to say.

It's impossible to watch the screen without a sense of futility. When you think about the soldiers and civilians, there is a sense of waste, as well.

They spend the next hour watching the bombs fall.

*

The party never seems to end, just as it never had a strict beginning. There is a sense, even past midnight, that no-one will ever be told to leave.

In the hall, in a moment of nothingness, his mobile phone vibrates in his pocket. On the screen is an unknown number. It would be difficult to hear the caller, in light of the music and the fact that one hundred people are enjoying themselves.

He puts the phone to his ear and says, 'Hello?'

When it comes, the voice is familiar. He should have known who it would be. The voice instructs him that he should visit Finsbury Park tomorrow.

'How come?'

'I've got some news that I think will interest you.'

Twenty-Four

The good thing is that he was able to set his terms. It was agreed that they should meet in Finsbury Park. More specifically, they agreed to meet at the railway bridge. All it requires is for him to wait.

There are lots of things surrounding him – trees, and such – but his mind is focused on something else. The feeling is that he mustn't be intimidated. He must get what he came for.

As soon as he reaches the bridge, he feels it necessary to lean on the edge. This seems like a sensible kind of camouflage. A passerby might mistake him for a trainspotter. You would never guess his presence on the bridge could have any greater significance.

What motivates him is a desire to close the chapter. There will be no mystery left. There will be nothing else to discover. Until then, it's not clear what he should expect. He has given up making predictions.

And then he doesn't have to think anymore, because he can see them approaching. He can see they're smiling. Margaret is mindful of the fact he is standing alone.

She looks older than he remembers. It's not that she hasn't made an effort. No, the hooped earrings tell you she's made plenty of effort. It's just that she looks quite old.

He is comfortable enough to shake Margaret's hand and do a half-kneel so that the little girl can say hello. It would be too weird to ruffle her hair.

'Say hello, Helen,' Margaret says.

The little girl is looking at a sparrow, which is pecking at a sugar sachet. She doesn't get up from her chair. This is a necessity of her affliction. Margaret is standing behind, keeping a firm grip on the handles. The one good thing about the press reports is that he learnt a lot about Helen. Her life has been determined by other people, which is something he can relate to. To think this little girl could be the subject of his misery is remarkable. She is looking at the sparrow, until it suddenly kicks its wings and flies.

Something still makes him worry. Does Helen know something? Has she remembered some secret unknown to him? You never know what he might have forgotten.

He must maintain a measure of composure. He could do a job of looking scared, but it wouldn't reflect how he feels. If the truth is on your side, nothing can go wrong. He knows himself to be a decent man, although he wouldn't credit himself with being anything more than decent.

Without waiting for any kind of cue, Margaret says, 'I'm sorry about all this.'

'Not at all.'

'Jim sends his regards.'

'Oh, good.'

'We never had any doubts.'

'I know.'

'We knew it was nonsense.'

'Yes, well. Not to worry.'

The little girl, Helen, is smiling at something. She is still too young to know what she's smiling about.

The bridge is what separates them from the track. It serves the purpose of being a sentimental place, and useful, as well. No-one would suspect they might be chatting about something untoward.

Margaret leans over the edge and says, 'Couldn't we have met somewhere else?'

'I like it here.'

'It's not exactly relaxing.'

Who would have thought that a train would pass underneath just as she said the words? It seems too good to be true. This is what happens, though.

It's important to change the subject. This is why he acknowledges the little girl with his hand and says, 'How's Helen getting on?'

Margaret says that Helen is getting on well, and that she took her out of school to attend this meeting.

'He insisted that it concerns both of us,' Margaret says.

Then Margaret asks how the family is.

Rosalind is fantastic, he explains. She has made a recovery. Muriel is also doing well, but has eliminated him from every aspect of her life.

'Oh, I'm sorry about that,' Margaret says. 'Still, it's good that you've done so well.'

Margaret mentions the guesthouse and how, when she saw it in a magazine, it made her think of him. She mentions some of his old colleagues, whose names he had almost forgotten, all of whom, she insists, were pleased to learn about Bevan Breakfast.

'Congratulations on your success,' she says.

If the words came from anyone else, he would be able to accept it. To Margaret, success might mean something different to what it ought to mean. Success, to her mind, is something that is always deserved. Whether it comes in monetary form, or some kind of acclaim, she wouldn't begrudge any of it. Do what you want, she would say. Nothing has any value unless it makes you rich, famous or adored.

It makes him wonder why they ever shared the same bed. It makes him sad on behalf of Helen, who might grow up to believe that meanness is a virtue. It makes him wonder if he should look out for Helen, as though she were his own child.

'Here we are,' comes the voice from behind, which causes them to turn around.

In his formal office suit, you immediately get the sense that Gideon has burdened himself by coming here. This is what Gideon looks like at work - a well-groomed horse, with a purposeful stride.

Gideon is holding a briefcase, which means nothing in itself. There are plenty of reasons why Gideon might carry a briefcase. It will be a busy day for Gideon, you suspect. There will be many more victims to apologise to. The briefcase will contain legal instructions on how to mitigate the worst lies.

Gideon has been keeping them waiting, but you wouldn't think there was anything rude about it. Gideon has perfected his professional smile.

'Thanks for coming,' Gideon says. 'It's good to get the three of you together.'

There is still a sense that Gideon isn't being his usual self. Everything would be different if Gideon were sitting at home, for instance, with his shirt and tie wrapped around the door. You have to remind yourself that Gideon wasn't born in an office.

'I've got some news,' Gideon says. 'It mostly concerns Joe, but I thought you might want to know, as well, Margaret.'

There is a change in Gideon's expression that suggests we are about to witness a certain level of seriousness. What is there to discuss? The fact that Gideon has taken time from his lunch hour suggests there is something important to say.

Gideon looks towards him and says, 'I've found out who it was.'

This is significant. This is what he wanted. You can tell it won't be good news, though. It will cause him pain.

'Who was it?'

'Well,' Gideon sighs, as if there is something big to consider. 'Do you remember when the story broke?'

'Yes.'

'And it came from an anonymous source.'

'That's right.'

This brings another sigh from Gideon.

'Let me explain. I was given the lead. I had no idea who it was.'

'Who was it?'

'I confronted the editor, and one of the lawyers.'

'And?'

'They told me about Barry Thorne.'

It's not so much said in words, but there's a conscious decision made that the four of them should look away.

Margaret is looking into the distance, as if she were respecting a minute's silence.

Gideon looks at him and mentions that Barry is not what he seems.

'I'm afraid you're one of his victims.'

The silence is all that's needed. There is no point in making a denial. He knows exactly what Barry is capable of. The silence is enough.

He has enough pride to say, 'I'm not a victim.'

Gideon has the intelligence to avoid sighing, and instead, begins to describe how Barry operates. There is a certain art to it, you see.

'The editor told me everything. Barry targets vulnerable public figures and invents stories about them. He's been doing it for years. Then – and this is the genius part – Barry contacts his own victims and offers a cheap PR service. Basically, he digs holes and gets paid to fill them in.'

'It's disgusting,' Margaret says. Then, when she puts on her empathy face, she touches his shoulder and says, 'Poor thing.'

'It's quite brilliant, really,' Gideon says. 'Half of Westminster are fighting stories he invented. It's like poisoning someone and charging them for the cure.'

'He just makes it all up?'

'Yes. Some of them turn out to be true, of course. He thought yours was plausible.'

It probably was plausible. You could easily believe he abandoned Helen, and everything else.

'It just escalated,' Gideon says. 'We got a call from a lady in Weston-super-Mare, who asked for more details. It was a hot story.'

'Weston-super-Mare?'

'If it's any consolation,' Gideon says, which means the next sentence will almost certainly be no consolation, 'you've done an extraordinary job in turning this around.'

It's no consolation. There is no reason to rejoice in defeat.

On a conscious level, he is aware of how unfortunate he is.

There are two ways in which he can react. He can react with anger or sadness. He would rather be angry, but sadness is inevitable. It's quite right that he should wallow. It's impossible to have a positive view. It doesn't account for the misery of the situation. What's the answer to his troubles? The answer will not come from the top of a railway bridge. But what should he do?

Gideon puts a hand on his back and says, 'Are you glad I told you?'

The answer is no, not really. You can hardly call it a relief. It's not as though he should punch the air. It makes him feel confused more than anything.

'I thought you should probably know about it,' Gideon says. 'You might want to file a lawsuit. We could get together all the other victims. Start a committee.'

'I don't care about that.'

'Then what are you going to do?'

'Reflect.'

Then at last, he is certain that everything is done. He is satisfied. There is no point in listening anymore. He is done, and now he can go home, wherever that is. Everything is fine. Yes, he is satisfied.

It's agreed between them – without it being said aloud – that it's time to go. Margaret uses her foot to prod the tilt lever. Together they go forward. A passerby would think that nothing bad had ever happened.

'Are you okay?' Margaret says.

He has no intention of answering. What motivates him is a desire to destroy something. That's what Rosalind would say. Just burn something. Burn all your troubles. In the absence of matchsticks, there is a problem. And where could he destroy something? It's just a wide open park with a playground, some tennis courts, and a path running through it. It's a shame that his mind is of the rational, thinking creature, not the spontaneous destroyer. He is excellent at doing things in a stupid way.

Helen wants to look at the pigeons, which are fighting over some bread. Margaret says there is not enough time.

Eventually they reach the gate. This is the beginning of the goodbye.

'Well, I'm glad it's all sorted,' Margaret says.

This is a strange thing to say. It doesn't feel like anything has been sorted.

'We can discuss what happens next.'

Then he begins to let his concentration slip.

There is nothing to think about. The world is turning without him.

Margaret and Gideon are responsible for the words. Whatever they're discussing is unimportant.

It's only the idiocy of their discussion that draws his attention.

Margaret, meaning to be innocuous, asks Gideon whether he has any tabloid gossip.

'I'm not a journalist anymore,' Gideon says.

This is interesting enough for him to re-engage with the conversation. He looks at Gideon and says, 'How come?'

'I wanted to start something new. I'm redeeming myself for twelve years of moral degradation.'

'So what are you doing now?'

'I'm a banker.'

There is no indication that Gideon is joking. It's difficult to know. It's probably best not to know, really.

Then Gideon offers a hand and wishes him the best of luck.

'You're a good man, Joe.'

It's hard to concentrate, which is what stops him from saying something nice. If he could concentrate, he would say thank you. He would try to smile. It's nice to meet someone honest, which admittedly means nothing. At least you can say that Gideon doesn't wish ill upon him. It will trouble him, later, that he hasn't said anything nice.

And Margaret, who he never loved, is able to give him a hug.

You don't imagine they will meet again. For it to happen, it would take another lie.

*

There is only one more thing, and then he's done.

Rosalind is the important thing. It's important to say goodbye, because he doesn't know when he will return. No-one can determine the future. All you can do is watch your life as a motion picture.

The studio door has been opened. The most surprising thing is that a new painting is hanging on the wall. Rosalind is looking at the canvas; she is pressing a finger against the page.

'It took me two hours,' Rosalind says, which is the same length of time he was absent.

She has managed to conjure something without going to exhaustive lengths.

The painting depicts the sea, with nothing to obscure the view. The swan is silhouetted on the horizon. The sunset makes a faint impression on the water. The power of the sun is diminishing.

Looking at the studio, he is unable to suppress his smile. All the things he remembers – the posters, the paint tins – have returned from their hiding place. It's as if Rosalind has reinstated them for nostalgia's sake. She has brought them out to make him happy. And to think they once irritated him!

She is alive, in so far as she is passionate again. She is creating things, where once she had only the ability to destroy. He would like to say well done, but it would sound condescending.

There is something surprising about what he feels. It's the possibility that he might, after all, be a success. Rosalind will flourish. He can claim some credit for that. He can claim one per cent.

It gives him hope that things could be different. It could all have been different, if the pendulum had swung the way it was supposed to. History has dealt him the worst cards.

She looks across from her painting and says, 'Do you want me to come with you?'

'It's alright. I think you should stay.'

It's difficult to know if he'll come back soon. He is unsure about what the agenda is. It seems wise that he should go somewhere else. The truth is that he doesn't belong anywhere.

On reflection, he should probably continue with the plan. The plan was to get away, wasn't it? What made him deviate from the plan? It was all the things that came in between. He just needs to keep going.

It's not anger that dominates him. His main feeling is a desire to get away. It would be tempting to visit Barry and ask for an explanation. It would require an energy he doesn't possess.

It's goodbye to the house, so long as Muriel is present. Rosalind can manage. Bevan Breakfast is a gift to her. She can share it with George.

The path he must tread is obvious. His mind is set.

The important thing is to keep walking. It requires him to exit the studio, and ignore the new arrival coming into the hall. There is just enough distance between himself and the guest to walk ahead unnoticed.

The rucksack is next to the shoes. It has been his biggest companion. It has followed him everywhere.

Rosalind is just behind and says, 'When are you back?'

'Soon.'

Rosalind mentions how she's making plans for the learning disabilities initiative. She is trying to find volunteers. It will occupy her thoughts for the next week.

Then she says, 'Why don't we do something nice one day?'

'Like what?'

'Something we'd both enjoy.'

Does such a thing exist? Between artwork and moaning, there is a chasm of difference.

'We could go for dinner,' Rosalind says.

Then, after a moment's reflection, he agrees that yes, it would be nice if they went for dinner. This is something they ought to do.

And then it comes to the moment when he has to decide how he should go. The temptation, of course, would be to make a drama of it. You could forgive him if he were to wave from the front garden gate. The departure should be simpler than that. It should be like any other exit. If necessary, they will hug at the front door, but this is dangerous. Doing such a thing would encourage him to think rationally for a moment. If he ever thought this way, he wouldn't be able to leave.

The door opens and nothing is said. There is nothing in the world he could say. His words would be inadequate. If only there was a visual way he could express his love. A teardrop, or something.

And then it's no surprise – but a delight all the same – to see Rosalind walking with him. Her smile is almost like a frown. She is wondering what he is looking so sad for.

All she can do is lift her arms around him. A hug is what he wanted, and he is glad to receive it.

He closes his eyes. It's the moment when he knows he must never let Rosalind go. This is probably what a father is supposed to feel. A father and daughter must never forget their love.

Twenty-Five

It's not inevitable that his story ends here, unless he should make it so.

When he thinks about the future he can only imagine a life alone with plants, spending days in a greenhouse, talking to vegetables. This is what the future will bring.

He never thought he would come back. It was never in the plan. Even at this precise moment, in his own living room, in front of his own television, there is not much satisfaction in being here.

Despite the journey, and the hours it took to return, he never felt alone until now. He never felt alone until it struck him, walking into the living room, that he doesn't belong here. It seemed like the only place left to come.

He lowers himself into the armchair. He lets his legs stretch out.

In front of him is the brick hearth and gas fire, which is switched on at the wall.

The dog is lying on its back. If he weren't so predisposed to hating the dog, he would consider it a true companion. The important thing is to keep a distance. It would be a mistake to fall in love with the dog.

On the journey, he had managed to drop his focus to the point where he didn't have to think. It was necessary to forget about the merits of the journey.

The best thing is that he's getting away. Does he belong here? Not really, but the house contains some important things. Most of his life has been shoved into the cellar. He would like to retrieve it.

He made the decision to come here, and what can you say about it? It would be natural to have regrets. Everything is a regret if you think about it for long enough. But still, there's no reason why the house shouldn't become his hiding place.

The hope is that Muriel will discover him. She will return from Bevan Breakfast. She will find him asleep on the sofa, in a position to be pitied. It might not happen, of course, but it's important to hope!

The sofa has served him well. The only thing he likes in the house is the sofa. No-one can disturb him. There is no need to rush anywhere. Time doesn't mean anything. He could sit here all morning and he still wouldn't know what to do. He has the two most beautiful things in the world - silence and no expectations.

At some point, though, he should get up. How long should he give it? In a perfect world, he would never have to do anything. If he could choose, his preference would be to fall asleep. Unfortunately, he has slept enough already. Sleep would give him a headache.

The longer he is alone, the more time he has to think. Of course, he would rather not have this time at all. It's impossible to think of all the months ahead and imagine how life could be different. What will the month of June bring? How will he feel in September? It's so far away. It's impossible to make plans for something that's so far in the future. And the criteria for his existence will be the same. Money must be raised from somewhere. Love will keep him sane and sometimes it will madden him. How do you control these things? It's best to assume that he will never have control.

*

At least he doesn't have to worry about making a noise when he walks around. In a normal situation, he would feel bad about making a noise, but he can admit to himself that no-one will care.

There is little to suggest the house was ever occupied by him, which of course, it was. It has the feel of a house that has been abandoned. The folk singer probably heard he was coming and decided to disappear. This is probably what happened.

The bedroom says something about Muriel, especially compared with the living room, which says nothing about anybody.

There is a desk on which she has laid some photographs and a piece of string. She has been making something. It will connect together when the string is threaded.

It's a relief to see the wedding photo on the chest of drawers. Muriel hasn't thrown the picture. It wouldn't have been a surprise, had she done so.

He pulls open the bedside drawer. It contains a hairdryer, which tells him nothing. It would have been better to see a note, or some reminder that she hasn't forgotten him.

In the en-suite bathroom is a wire from which some photographs are hanging dry. The room is ventilated with an extractor fan. The chemicals are labelled to differentiate them from the shampoo. There is a black bin bag taped across the window. There is a strip of wood that blocks any light seeping through the door. The room is light proof. She has managed to make it so there is complete darkness.

There is something to do. What exactly did he come upstairs for? He was looking for something. There is a list of things he ought to pack, just in the event that he should leave, and never return.

It will bore him to pack his things. He doesn't want to feel bored. He wants to live for a reason. It's the trivial things that make him feel defeated. It's the thought of having to lift things into a bag.

No, there is nothing to do. At most, he can whittle it down to a list of two things. He could get up and walk, or he could fall asleep. It's only now – at the thought of sleeping – that he's able to rouse himself and wonder if he should let the light in.

*

The kitchen is enough to make you laugh. It has been beyond his ambition just to clean the dirty plates. The best thing would be to hire a van, drive to a cliff and throw it all into the sea. That would be the best thing.

With his finger he can feel that the tap water is cold. It should only take a moment to get warm, but the moment has gone. Will it be necessary to call the boiler man? He would rather have a cold shower if it means he doesn't have to call the boiler man. Of course, he could pull open the cupboard and check the meter, but he'd rather just presume it's all broken.

He flicks on the kettle, just for the noise.

It won't be long until the dirty plates begin to mount. Everything will get dirtier. The house will be impossible to live inside. He will need to move to another house, or drive his house to the cliff and throw it into the sea.

It's only when the pot of tea has brewed, and he begins to pour it into his mug, that he realises something. It has troubled him for longer than he imagined it would. It's impossible to get rid of the thought. It's still in his mind. It's just as bad as when he first thought about it.

Imagine if Barry had never invented the lie.

Would life have been different? Would Muriel still love him? Is it right to assume they would have carried on living together? It's necessary, of course, to believe things would have been exactly the same. To think things might have been different is not something worth imagining. It would immobilise him, were he to think too much. He must think of something better, or think of nothing at all.

In an hour or so, things will be impossible. Just imagine - an hour of sitting at the kitchen table, or staring through the window. It will have a damaging effect.

It's time to get out. It's time to get outside and see what happens. Wilful abandon, you could call it.

The next important thing is to search for the key, which he is able to do by patting the pockets of his jeans. Nothing else, except his coat, is important.

He pulls down his coat from the hook.

It would be a risk to go outside, given the rain clouds, but it doesn't matter. There is enough daylight for him to see everything. It would be better to walk now, when the streets are deserted, than to wait until midday.

He pulls up his zip. He pulls up his collar.

It's better to walk at this time. The alternative is to sit indoors, and wait for someone who might never come.

He had almost forgotten about the dog. Its front end is lowered, almost as an invitation to pat its head. The dog is dependable. The dog is loyal. You can see why Muriel has fallen in love with Bruno.

It's just by instinct that he looks over his shoulder as if to say goodbye. And it's instinct, too, that demands he should shut the door quickly.

It's not clear what purpose he has in coming outside. It's not like he woke up and decided to do it. It's just that he didn't want to be alone. And of course, now that he's walking down the street, it's possible that anything could happen. He could fall in love! Something can happen, at least. Nothing could happen if he were to sit indoors. There is lots of time for something to happen. It will come.

The only trouble is the ugliness of everything. If he thinks about the buildings in front of him, it won't do him any good. It makes him think that he's crazy to be here. Sometimes, without warning, he'll look at the buildings and he'll start to think too much. It'll go something like, why am I here? And then if he takes it further, he'll try and justify all the decisions that brought him here. Most of the time, he can't think of an excuse.

The sun is beginning to rise, not that you can even see it. In this town, the sun is just a concept. You know it exists, but it's not often you see it. At least his coat pockets are deep enough for him to bury his hands. It keeps him warm, at least.

Just beyond the iron bridge is the broken pub. If he had the money, it would be nice to refurbish it, just out of kindness, rather than any business rationale.

It's only when he steps down to the beach that he has an idea of where to go. The best thing is to walk, and wait for something to happen. The force of the wind doesn't matter, because no-one can see his flattened hair.

If you were visiting the beach for the first time, you wouldn't think much of the view. It's only after the one hundredth visit that you appreciate the scale of everything.

What he likes about the beach is the lack of sand. You don't have to worry about your toenails. There is little else to recommend the beach.

On the concrete walkway is a large, padlocked shed where the rowing boats are kept. It's just a rotting lean-to shed, and the padlock is rusting.

He pulls at the padlock to see if it will give an inch.

The door is loosened so you can see inside. There is enough light to see the pedalos. One of them is shaped like a swan! Say he were to ride a pedalo - what's the harm?

There must be some way in which he could get inside. A rock would do it. The best thing he can see is a stone. He retrieves the stone.

How should he do it? With the stone he could hit the lock near the shackle holes. A couple of firm blows would do it. Then, after a dozen blows, the rusty seal will give way. That's how he should do it.

He looks closer and can definitely see that one of the pedalos is a giant swan. It has a long neck with a mini-slide attached to the stern.

From the lock he wipes whatever rust he can.

It wouldn't be nice, necessarily, to strike the lock with such force. Is it the only way to get inside? It might be possible to get the pedalo in a more legitimate way. The more he thinks about it, the more he doesn't want to break the shed. Is there an alternative? There must be another way. It's true that some of the pedalos are kept in the shed, but where else? If he remembers correctly, you can rent a boat at the foot of the pier.

The momentum is what leads him forward.

Underneath the pier is the line of boats. Some of them are rowing boats, and some of them are pedalos.

At the sea wall you can see the old man, who is standing behind a sign. You can rent a boat for a fiver.

Then he asks the man – pleads, almost – whether he could ride a pedalo.

'Take your pick,' the old man says.

There are rowing boats – about eight of them – and a few pedalos. None of them are shaped like a swan. None of them have a slide attached to the stern.

'I want a swan.'

'We don't have any.'

'Yes you do. I saw one.' Then he opens his wallet and removes ten pounds. He says, 'I want a swan.'

'Why?'

'I like swans.'

The old man looks at the wallet. You can tell what the old man is thinking. Why is a swan pedalo worth ten pounds?

There is nothing about the man to suggest he knows anything about boats. It's just that ten pounds is too much to turn down for a swan pedalo ride.

Without anything being said, he is encouraged to follow the man down to the shed. There is something exciting about this.

'This is it,' the old man says, removing some keys from his pocket.

It doesn't take long before the lock is freed and the shed draws open. It contains a number of useful things. On the shelf are a couple of paint pots. There is a stack of folded beach chairs.

In the light you can see the swan pedalo.

With a heave, the two of them hoist the thing. It's an effort just to carry it an inch.

At the midway point, between the shed and the water's edge, you can see the old man shaking his head. It would be too much to drag it all back. It would require too much energy.

The old man gestures for him to step onto the small wooden deck, which stretches a couple of feet into the water. With his foot, the old man positions the rudder so that it doesn't scrape on the shingles. The pedalo is positioned in the water. From here it's possible to let go.

'You've got forty-five minutes,' the old man says.

It's a big swan-shaped pedalo. It has a shallow, rounded bottom, which makes it difficult to step inside. When he positions himself in the driver's seat it's noticeable how light everything is. You can almost feel yourself bouncing on the waves.

The pedalo is not quite positioned right, because he's still sorting out his feet. It's only when he puts his foot down on the pedals that he feels like he's going somewhere.

The journey has begun, and he's glad that he doesn't have a map. The pedalo could take him somewhere, and this is the beautiful thing. If he were to pedal in a straight line, where would he reach? Norway, perhaps.

It would be a mistake to look at the horizon and try to make something of it. It's better to leave the horizon alone. And besides, the beauty is not so much what he can see, as it is what he can escape from.

There are no boats on the water, so he doesn't have to think about what he's doing. In the distance is a tanker, but nothing else. The thing that delights him most is the idea of silence. It's not silent yet, but it will be.

He looks over his shoulder, and can see the old man giving a wave. Goodbye, stranger. In all probability, the old man won't see another customer for hours. It's quite likely that the man will be standing on the beach for a long time.

The relaxing thing about a pedalo is that you can stop pedalling after a while. You can do what you want. You can even lean back in the seat and stretch your arms! At the same time, could he not have brought some food along? It's a shame he didn't make something. His wisdom tooth was hurting. It has required him to eat soft foods, like an elephant in its dying days on the swamp. It might be the case that he's been grinding his teeth in his sleep, but no-one can verify this.

In a short while he will bring himself to smile. It's right that he should smile, because no-one can see him. It's a good thing that no-one can see him. A very good thing, and sort of unexpected. It's good, as well, that he's able to look up and see a clear sky. It has been a while since the sky was clear. He is glad about the weather, and glad to be alone.

Just in front of the cockpit is a little deck, where you could stand if you wanted to be brave. If he could get away with it, he would stand up. It would be good to stand up, just because he can.

He is able to position his feet on what they call the hull.

Then he puts his arms in the air. Just beneath, you can feel a rocking sensation.

There is a lot to think about all at once, like how to keep your balance and where to position your feet.

If he could put his hand to his head, it would make him laugh. He could do a salute! But what would he salute for? It would make him laugh, as much as anything.

Just as he thought, the salute makes him laugh aloud. It has a maddening effect, which he can feel. It makes him feel like he can do anything. Why not jump in the water?

It's true that he hadn't expected the sea to make such an impression. It seemed more likely that he would see it for what it is - a vast, boring expanse with nothing much to recommend it. But he had forgotten something. The sea belongs to him.

There is no reason to be afraid. He could handle a storm or

simply let it wash over him. The wind will be a challenge. The cold will keep him alert. A number of things could happen, none of which are frightening. Nothing will capsize him.

The water is dark when you pedal further out. You don't have to turn around to know that the town is a long way back. Something has been accomplished. Without being certain, the journey has been longer than forty-five minutes. It's a shame that he needs to disappoint the old man. This is the price of freedom.

If he lets his eyes close then he doesn't have to think about anything. It's possible that he could fall asleep, which is something to be glad about. If he wanted, he could position his legs overboard. The pedalo is strong enough to remain waterborne. He wouldn't want to put money on it, but the pedalo is strong enough. All you need is a direction, which is a straight line forward. It's better to continue in a straight line. It feels like the best thing. Just keep going in a straight line, and it doesn't matter where it ends. The line can go on for as long as it wants. In the ocean, there are no traffic lights. Nothing could make him so calm as the sight of an ocean all to himself.

Acknowledgements

I'd like to thank all the team at Legend Press, in particular Lauren Parsons for supporting the novel and for being a thoughtful and judicious editor.

A big thanks to my agent Wendy Scozzaro at Felix de Wolfe for her continued guidance and for taking a punt. I will pay for lunch one day.

Thank you to Furious D and Madge for setting an example of openness, love, artistic integrity and abysmal cooking. Elizabeth, Eddy the Iceman and T, you have been the finest siblings a purr-pig could ever wish for.

To Sarah Jack, my partner and lobster, thank you for being my first reader.

Mark Gill - thanks for your insight, friendship, and for showing me how to sleep on a living room floor using only sofa cushions.

Thanks also to the common room at Fortismere School, my tutors at Lancaster and Manchester Universities, and everyone who's taken the time to read my work and told me not just what I want to hear - 'you're brilliant' - but what I need to know ('you're brilliant').

Come and visit us at
www.legendpress.co.uk

Follow us
@legend_press